D0007998

DAWN OF FEAR

Books by Susan Cooper available in Collier Books editions:

THE DARK IS RISING SEQUENCE
Over Sea, Under Stone
The Dark Is Rising
Greenwitch
The Grey King
Silver on the Tree
Seaward

DAWN OF FEAR

BY

Susan Cooper

Illustrated by Margery Gill

ALADDIN BOOKS
MACMILLAN PUBLISHING COMPANY NEW YORK

Aladdin Books
Macmillan Publishing Company
866 Third Avenue, New York, NY 10022
Collier Macmillan Canada, Inc.
First Aladdin Books edition 1989
Published by arrangement with Harcourt Brace Jovanovich, Inc.
Printed in the United States of America

10 9 8 7 6 5 4 3 2 1

Library of Congress Cataloging-in-Publication Data
Cooper, Susan.
Dawn of fear / Susan Cooper; illustrated by Margery Gill.—1st Aladdin Books ed.
p. cm.
Summary: Three English children, fascinated by the war air raids, gradually become aware of true fear and horror when they seek vengeance on an opposing gang that destroyed their hideaway.
ISBN 0-689-71327-4
1. World War, 1939–1945—Great Britain—Juvenile fiction. [1. World War, 1939–1945—Great Britain—Fiction. 2. Gangs—Fiction.] I. Gill, Margery, ill. II. Title
PZ7.C7878Daw 1989
[Fic]—dc20 89-6820 CIP AC

for Rod

Contents

DAWN OF FEAR

1

Friday

The air-raid siren went at the beginning of the afternoon, in an English lesson, while Mrs. Wilson was reading them "Children of the New Forest." At first they couldn't hear the siren at all for the school whistles: a chorus of alarm, their own indoor warning, shrilling down all the corridors at once.

"Ma'am, ma'am! A raid, ma'am!"

Mrs. Wilson closed the book with a deliberate snap and stood up. "All right now, children, quickly and quietly. Books in your desks, take out your gas masks, all stand up. Anybody not got his gas mask? Very good. Now I want a nice neat line to the shelter, and no running."

A hand was waving wildly at the front of the class. "Ma'am, is it a real raid, ma'am?"

"It's a drill," said a scornful voice.

"It's the wrong time for a drill."

Mrs. Wilson scowled, and they knew the scowl and were quiet. "We don't know yet. Door monitor?"

Little Albert Russell was already stiff at attention by the open door, the strap of his gas-mask case neat across his chest. Out they went into the corridor, from one row of desks at a time, their double file jostling the filing classes from the other rooms, out to the air-raid shelters in the playground.

Derek and Peter had desks near the classroom window. Geoffrey was behind them.

"Can you see anything?"

"Nah. Hear the siren now, though. Listen."

The head-splitting school whistles had stopped, and Derek listened as he walked, and heard the distant wail of the siren rise and fall until they were down the corridor and going out of the big double door. He and Peter and Geoff were nearly at the end of the line; Mrs. Wilson was counting heads just in front of them. He shivered; the sun was shining through broken clouds, but there was a chill wind. Most of the other classes, the younger ones, were made to take their overcoats into the shelters, but his group, the farthest from the cloakrooms, had no time ever to fetch theirs.

He became conscious suddenly of the drone of engines somewhere high up.

"Look!" Peter stopped, excited, pointing.

The three couples behind them fell over their feet as he stopped, and then skirted him and went nervously, disapprovingly on. Only Geoffrey paused. The girl who had been walking with him called over her shoulder, "Come *on,*" but she was Susan Simmons, who was always bossy, and the boys took no notice, but stood where they were and stared up.

Where Peter was pointing, there was a pattern of

slow-moving dots in the sky. The deep hum of the engines grew as he watched, and developed a kind of throbbing sound. The clouds were very high, and the planes were flying below them; they seemed light-colored and were not easy to see unless the sun went behind a cloud. Their noise seemed so loud now that Derek looked all around the rest of the sky for more, but saw nothing except the familiar floating shapes of the seven barrage balloons, three near, four far off, fat silver ovals hanging up there with bulbous fins at their tails, like great friendly bloated fish. The balloons were filled with hydrogen, he knew, and tethered by thick cables; they were there to get in the way of any Nazi pilot coming in low to drop his bombs.

"Junkers," Geoffrey said confidently. "Junker eighty-eights."

What with his own excitement and the height of the formation, Derek could not really make out the silhouette of any individual plane; but by the same token he knew that Geoff couldn't either. "No, no," he said. "Dorniers."

And then in the second that they still paused on the black asphalt playground, with the grubby concrete boxes that were the air-raid shelters looming ahead of them, they saw the unbelievable happen. Suddenly the rigid, steadily advancing formation of enemy planes broke its pattern, lost its head as plane after plane broke away and dived; and they heard a new higher noise and glimpsed, diving through a broad gap in the clouds out of the sun, a gaggle of other smaller planes scattering the bombers as a dog scatters sheep. It was a furious sky now, full of coughing gunfire.

They heard other guns open up, deeper, closer, on the ground.

"Gosh!" Derek said. He had forgotten entirely where he was; he hopped in delight. His gas-mask case banged at his back. *"Gosh!"*

"Fighters, our fighters!" Peter waved madly at the sky. "Look!"

And they were lost in breathless looking and in the growing scream of engines and the thumping of gun-fire, as an urgent hand came down and Mrs. Wilson dragged them off toward the shelter.

"You *stupid* boys, come under cover *at once*!" Her voice was a squeak of anxious rage, and it was only the realization that she was angrier than they had ever seen her that brought them skidding into the entrance to the shelter. But even then Peter was still staring back over his shoulder, and all at once he let out a yell of such joyful surprise that all four of them, even Mrs. Wilson, paused, hypnotized, for a last glimpse of the sky.

"He's got him, he's got him, he's got him!"

It was a Hurricane—Derek could see the blunt nose now—and it had dived after one of the weaving bomb-ers, with its guns making bright flashes on its wings. And the bomber had been hit: it was trailing a ragged path of black smoke behind it and lurching erratically across the sky and down. It was still firing its guns; you could hear them and see them among the puffs of smoke in the sky that were the bursts of shells fired from the ground. Nearer and nearer the ground the plane came, a long way away from them but still visible, and as it dived, it veered close to one of the motionless

silver barrage balloons, and suddenly there was a sound like a soft "whoomph" and a great burst of flame.

The plane dropped and vanished, with the victorious Hurricane above it swooping off to join the battle that they could still hear but no longer see; the sound of the crash was no more than a faraway thump, like the firing of one of the anti-aircraft guns, but enough to galvanize Mrs. Wilson into thrusting them ahead of her around the right-angle bend of the entrance into the shelter itself. But still Derek had one moment's last quick sight over his shoulder of the burning barrage balloon, hanging there in the sky as it always had but beginning strangely to droop, with its fat inflated fins no longer sticking firmly out but curving gently, wearily, down.

When they came out of the shelter about half an hour later, the barrage balloon was no longer there. Instead, there was a gap in the sky and only six floating guardian shapes. The raid had not lasted for very long; there had been time for a handful of songs—the fourth- and fifth-grade children in their shelters had been singing "Waltzing Matilda" when they came in—and the distribution of one hard candy each. Then the noise outside, which they heard only in the brief gap between one song and the next, had died away, and the long single note of the "all clear" had shrilled out. They went back to their classrooms, in as neat a double file as before, and smartie Susan Simmons made a shocked face at Derek and Peter and Geoff and whispered to her friends as they passed.

The three boys stayed after school, hovering at their desks until everyone else had left, to apologize to Mrs. Wilson, and curiously she did no more than give them a brief lecture on the perils of being out in the open when a raid was on, and the undeniable extra crime of giving someone else the risk of coming to haul them inside.

"She's nice," Derek said on the way home. "I mean, she could have sent us to the principal, and then they'd have told our parents, and there'd have been an awful row."

"She ought to be grateful, if you ask me," Peter said. "If she hadn't had to come and find us, she'd have missed all the fun."

2

Saturday

"We got a new shelter," Peter said, balancing on his heels on the low brick wall in the way all their parents forbade. Every house in the small road had this same brick wall enclosing its front garden: a sitting-height wall, topped with curved tile, and a chunky iron chain looped between concrete posts above that. The iron chains were supposed to go one day to the War Effort, but nobody ever came to take them away.

"Where is it?"

"In the dining room. It's an indoors one. Under the table."

"Go on. No such thing."

"It is. Come and see."

They ran down the road, dodging puddles, kicking stones, jumping vainly to catch at blossoms on the fluffy pink cherry trees. No one seemed to look after the trees in the road, but every spring it happened: the dark red buds burst into a froth of pink cotton wool, later to shed petals and brown rotting flowers on the patches of grass outside each house. Peter bounded past one tree, stumbled, and spun around clutching his foot and yelping.

"What's up?"

"Stubbed my toe. Damn, damn, damn."

Geoffrey said primly, "You aren't supposed to say that."

"Chickory chick, cha-la, cha-la," Peter sang mockingly at him. "Chickory chick . . ."

Geoff did look a bit like a chicken sometimes, Derek reflected, with that pointy nose and the curly dark hair like feathers. He said, in experiment, "Cluck, cluck. Nice chickie."

"Shut up!" Geoffrey aimed a furious punch at his stomach, and Derek groaned, staggered, clutching himself, hopping in circles. Geoffrey looked pleased. Derek burst into laughter.

"Come on then."

They whirled through Peter's gate, through the front garden, past the hawthorn tree with its dark red blossoms already beginning to break, around to the back door where Mrs. Hutchins was shaking out a rug, raising a cloud of glinting dust in the sunshine. At another house they might have hawked and coughed and howled at the dust, but Mrs. Hutchins was unpredictable. She was small and neat-featured, with her fair hair wisping out in all directions; she had blue eyes as bright as Peter's, but did not laugh as he did. Most of the time she seemed to Derek to be either neutral, putting up with everything, or complaining.

She said at once to Peter when she saw them, "Have you been in Miss Mac's room again?"

Miss MacDonald was the lodger, an elderly teacher. There were lodgers at Derek's house, too, though they had just gone away for a week's holiday. Most of the houses in the road now had extra people living in them besides the family.

"No, Mum," Peter said.

"There's a vase broken," Mrs. Hutchins said, looking at him keenly. Her gaze swept over the others, too, as if she suspected them of having crept in and broken the vase. Derek shuffled uncomfortably. Finally she looked away vaguely and gave her rug a last vigorous shake.

"Can I show them the shelter, Mum?"

"She'll say no," Derek thought. "She'll say: Certainly not, I don't want you all tramping in dirt when I'm cleaning. She'll say: Our new shelter is private."

But Mrs. Hutchins smiled faintly, lifted her chin, and tucked a wisp of hair back beside one ear. "The Morrison?" she said. "All right. Wipe your feet, now."

It looked like a huge box filling the space under the dining-room table. When Derek looked more closely, he saw that it was really a kind of table itself, made of steel, but with the space between its thick steel legs filled in on all four sides by walls of heavy wire mesh. There was an entrance at one end. It was like a small house, or a camp; it would make a good camp. No one could attack it. You could sit inside and laugh at them.

"It's smashing," he said enviously.

"I expect we're getting one, too," Geoffrey said. There was no air-raid shelter at his house; when the warning came, he and his parents went down into the shelter next door.

"Bet you aren't."

"Bet we are."

"We take the cat inside, too," Peter said. "We all go to sleep. It's warm. We were in there last night."

Derek thought of last night, but could not find it. He felt a vague memory of his father carrying him, half asleep, outside—but when was that, last night or another? There were too many such nights to know.

He looked again at the heavy metal Morrison, into which Peter had now crawled to sit grinning up at them, and decided he preferred their own. At home, the air-raid shelter was in the back garden; a truck had delivered pieces of shining silvery corrugated iron of different shapes, some flat rectangles and some curved, and his father and Uncle Bob, the lodger, had dug a huge hole in the back lawn and built the small house that was the shelter, covering it afterwards with earth and grass so that it looked like a large bump in the lawn. There was a wall of sandbags in front of the doorway, and to get in, you climbed down on one side of them, into a trench. The floor was earth, damp sometimes, covered with sacks; there were four bunks and a smell of gardens. He slept in a top bunk, which was, yes, far more interesting than the Hutchinses' table-cave.

"Outside, Peter," Mrs. Hutchins said, appearing at the door. "I want to get tea; your father'll be home soon." She had a way of addressing all her remarks to her son, over the heads of the others, as if they were not there. Derek's mother had once said Mrs. Hutchins was shy. He did not see how this was possible, which was why he had remembered it.

"I like your shelter, Mrs. Hutchins," he said, looking at her.

"Yes," she said. "It's one of the first. Mr. Hutchins got it through his firm." But she smiled at him, and he thought that she looked pretty when the lines of her face went up instead of down.

They went out into the back garden, and a bird flew away from the birdbath that stood like a concrete mushroom in the middle of the lawn. Derek stared into the docile pool of water; it was dark green, with a broken snail shell at the bottom.

"Let's go and feed the chickens," said Geoffrey. He fished out the snail shell and threw it at the base of the birdbath; it smashed and scattered, leaving a small wet mark.

"Look here a minute," Peter said. "In the garage. I got something for the camp. For the Ditch."

He pushed open the garage door. "See—we can use them to keep up the roof when we've dug the hole. Like in mining. So the earth won't collapse." He showed them two packing cases made of a thin white wood, and they stared. They had never seen packing cases, only the cardboard boxes that the grocer sometimes relinquished to hold the cans and packages that their mothers brought home. And the cardboard boxes were precious enough; hoarded like treasure, to be used over and over again.

"Where'd you get them?"

Peter grinned. "They're my dad's. But he won't mind."

"Have you asked him?" Derek said doubtfully.

"He won't mind," Peter said again, and laughed. He

was an unworried boy, more often in trouble than any of them, but always a carefree kind of trouble. Derek liked him better than he did Geoffrey. You could be sure of Pete; he wouldn't ever shove you from behind unexpectedly or say spiteful things; and once when they had all three torn a curtain in Derek's house, Pete had gone straight to Mrs. Brand and taken the blame, with Derek trailing guiltily behind. But Geoff had run home.

"Pet—er!" His mother was calling. "Come in now."

"I better go to tea, too," Geoffrey said. "Those boxes are good."

"We'll start digging tomorrow," Peter said to Derek. "Come and call for you in the morning, all right?"

"All right."

Geoffrey ran across the road to his own house, and Derek wandered home, weaving in and out between the puddles, as near as he could get to the middle of the road. No cars were likely to interrupt him; there was little traffic in the small world of Everett Avenue, except bicycles. It was a private road, leading nowhere, and altogether unpaved save for its curbstones and drains; a stony road, a quiet turning off the main highway, ending abruptly in a field. Beyond the field, the Great Western Railway stretched across the horizon, so that life in Everett Avenue was accompanied by the murmur of cars on the highway at one end, and the distant roar of trains at the other.

From the field that lay between the road and the railway came a raucous noise, suddenly: the hollow, off-key tapping of metal on baked clay, a hammer on a pipe. Clear and rhythmic, it went on for perhaps half a minute. Derek stopped beside his gate and stood listening. The tapping meant that he must run indoors; but after all he was nearly there already. It came, he knew, from the anti-aircraft post in the field beyond the top of the road; there were guns up there, and soldiers, and sandbags, but all in mysterious isolation, for everything was fenced in with barbed wire, and the boys had never been able to get close. The tapping on the pipe usually foretold an air raid; and a few moments later the warning for everybody else, the long wailing up-and-down siren, would rise into the sky. But as Derek stood there listening now and found nothing following but silence, he knew that this was one of the other times, when the tapping meant nothing very important at all. It was simply calling the soldiers to come and have their tea.

Tea. He shut the gate and ran indoors. His mother was carrying plates into the front room. "You can take some if you don't drop them," she said. "One at a time."

Derek took—one at a time—the knobby white milk jug, the pot of plum jam, the breadboard with its rectangular grayish-faced loaf of bread. He saw his mother take a certain handleless cup from the larder. "Toast?" he said hopefully. "And dripping?"

"I shouldn't be surprised," said Mrs. Brand, smiling. "I didn't mean to light the fire, with coal so short, but Hugh was cold. Go on back in, now, or he'll be up to mischief."

Back in the living room, Derek kept his small brother at bay and unhooked the brass toasting fork that hung beside the fireplace; he knew the bread would crumble if he tried to spear it properly, but he could let it hang suspended by its top crust from the prongs—while his mother, using an ordinary short fork, toasted three pieces of bread to his one.

"They've got a new shelter at Peter's house," he said. "It's under the table; it's funny. Not so nice as ours. Mrs. Hutchins said it was a Mosson."

"Morrison," Mrs. Brand said absently. She looked at small Hugh, playing happily with a spoon. "Too late for us to have one, now we've got the Anderson outdoors. It would have been better for Hughie's cough, though. Getting him up every night to go out there in the cold. . . ." She sighed. "Ah, well."

She spread Derek's toast with the granular brown dripping from the kitchen cup, and sprinkled it with salt. He munched contentedly, gazing into the fire. Castles in there: battlements and towers golden-red and glowing; suddenly, a leering face; then as suddenly nothing, but only a patch of tar and a tiny spurting yellow flame. He said, "Can I poke the fire?"

"It doesn't need it, darling. You can't make toast with flames."

"When's Daddy coming home?"

"Soon. After 'Children's Hour.' "

"A boy at school said they're bombing the railways out of London every night now," Derek said.

Mrs. Brand was silent for a moment. Then she said firmly, "You don't want to believe everything you hear from the boys at school."

"Why is Daddy working on a Saturday?"

"He has to sometimes, you know that, when there's lots of work to do at the office."

" 'Children's Hour,' " said Hugh. He was guessing, but he was right; it was nearly five o'clock. Derek turned on the radio. "These sets take a long time to warm up," he said, quoting a current catchphrase. "Eeeeee-ow yip-pip-pip-pip-pip . . ."

The radio set added a squeal of its own, and his mother laughed.

"Hello, children," said the familiar disembodied voice. "To begin our program today, David is going to read you one of the *Just So Stories* by Rudyard Kipling, the story of 'The Cat That Walked by Himself.' "

Hear and attend and listen; for this befell and behappened and became and was, O my Best Beloved, when the Tame animals were wild. And Derek and Hugh attended and listened, eating a rock cake each, while their mother cleared the dirty plates and went into the kitchen to boil water for tea and open a can of baked beans in case the five-twenty train from Paddington might this one evening be on time. Hugh was lost in the story, staring into the fire. Derek was half listening, half brooding on where they should begin building their camp in the Ditch tomorrow. *"Cat, come with me." "Nenni!" said the Cat. "I am the Cat who walks by himself, and all places are alike to me . . ."* And in their quiet room with the darkening windows, the story drew on and was followed by a play and some gentle music. Then, "Good night, children, everywhere," said the familiar voice, and they answered it: "Good night." And after the weather forecast the news began, "And this is Stuart Hibberd reading it," and in the middle of the talk about troops and airplanes and fronts that Derek could never properly understand, their father came home. Hugh was put to bed while John Brand ate his baked beans on toast, and shortly afterwards Derek followed him, into the room where they all four now slept and where the boys would hear the low murmur of voices and perhaps the radio, comfortingly close, until they fell asleep. It was an ordinary day.

But late that night, Derek woke. He woke into a confusion of sound; Hugh was whimpering in his cot across the room, with his mother bent over to comfort him, and thunder was rumbling in the night outside. Or perhaps it was not thunder. He said sleepily, "Are we going down the shelter?"

His father's voice said, "Not yet. Go to sleep," and he saw that John Brand was standing near the window in the dark, looking out, with the blackout curtain held open, and that the dim light in the room came not from the hall but from the sky outside. He wondered why; and half asleep but puzzled, he sat up in bed. The thunder growled and died. His father looked across at him and said in a strange, tight voice, "You might as well have a look."

Derek clambered across the foot of his bed toward him. Even without the blackout curtains, it would have been a dark room, for two large wardrobes were set across the French windows as a protection against broken glass. But in the place where his father stood, you could see out of a window, through the apple trees in the garden, and over the fence to the eastern horizon. Lightning was still flickering at one side of the sky, but it was a small local storm and moving quickly away. Derek felt vaguely that his father had not been looking at the storm. He gazed ahead through the gap in the trees, to where the searchlights were making their usual weaving crisscross pattern in the sky, blind white groping arms sweeping to and fro. And he saw suddenly that below the searchlights the sky above the horizon was red.

There in the east, it glowed with a reddish-orange haze he did not remember having seen before, like a strange misplaced sunset, glowing in the night sky. "What's that?" he said.

His mother had quieted Hugh and come up behind them, and when she spoke, there was the same curious, taut note that he had heard in his father's voice.

"That's London, burning," she said.

His parents, Derek knew, were Londoners. After they were married, they had moved twenty miles out of London to the flat green valley of the Thames. Everett Avenue had been newly built then, and there in the peaceful road with the view of Lombardy poplars and golden fields, he and Hugh had been born. *That's London, burning.* Derek could not picture what it meant. He supposed, looking out at that red band in the sky, that the Jerries had dropped a lot of bombs again and set things on fire. That was not remarkable. They had been dropping bombs for ages now; it was only a shame that nothing so colorful as a fire ever happened really near home. Still, at least they had seen that super dogfight yesterday and the spectacular collapse of that poor old balloon. It wasn't often you got a piece of luck like that when the bombers came. "They aren't near us tonight," he thought wisely. "You can't hear the guns."

He climbed back into his bed, pulled the blankets around his ears, and drifted away toward sleep. Dimly through the muffling bedclothes he heard his parents talking softly as they covered the windows again and prepared for bed.

"The city again. Or the docks. Poor devils. I didn't think there'd be one tonight."

"He's throwing over everything he's got now."

"In a way we're lucky the boys are so young. Even to Derry it doesn't mean much. Just a great game, like cowboys and Indians. It's hard—you have to teach them to be careful, yet you don't want to teach them to be afraid."

"I hope to God," John Brand said somberly, "nothing will happen to make him learn that for himself."

Snug among his blankets, Derek wondered vaguely what he could mean; and then the warmth and the darkness took him, and it was too much effort even to wonder. And he fell asleep.

3

Sunday

There was porridge for breakfast. Derek sprinkled sugar over the top, watching it dissolve into a watery syrup, and carefully poured on just enough milk to make a white moat all around the dish, cooling and firming the edges of the secure gray-white island that he would invade with his spoon. You could make bays, and rivers, before you ate them. Sometime he would teach Hugh.

Outside the window, sunlight whitened the big cherry tree by the front gate, and the sky above the houses across the road was clear blue. School tomorrow, but not today. He said, "Can I go over the Ditch, Mum?"

She said, smiling, "I'll tell Peter where to find you."

It was not far; the Ditch lay along the other side of the Robinsons next door, where the vanished builder Mr. Everett had intended to put another road, crossing Everett Avenue at right angles, but had been interrupted by the war. He had had time to build only the first half of this other road, which now stretched off on the far side of Everett Avenue like a side arm, opposite the Ditch. It was called Woodland Drive, but never known to the people of Everett Avenue as anything but the White Road. Almost white it was, too, paved in broad concrete sections joined together by black asphalt lines. There was little or no contact between the residents of the two roads, though nobody seemed to know why.

The half-dozen Woodland Drive children made up an independent gang, and Peter, Derek, and Geoffrey referred to them formally as the Children from the White Road. The two groups had never clashed, but they avoided one another. The invisible gang boundary ran across the near end of the White Road, and the Everett Avenue boys stayed on their own side of it, in Everett Avenue itself and the Ditch. The Children from the White Road seldom trespassed there, but remained in unseen haunts of their own.

Derek turned right, past the Robinsons' front wall, into the Ditch. None of them had ever thought of it as anything but a natural feature of the landscape; it had been there as long as they had, and that was forever. To anyone else, no doubt, it was obviously the beginnings of a road, because of its width, stretching between the two solid creosoted fences of the Robinsons' and the Twyfords' house just beyond, and because of the eight-foot-deep central trench dug to take pipes that had never arrived. But for the boys, the Ditch had no purpose but their own. The pipe-trench had widened over the years into a miniature valley, with a path on either side running precariously along the ridges cast up when the earth had first been dug out; hardly earth, really, but orange-brown clay. In summer it hardened into a brick-like substance reamed by cracks and fissures, cloudy with orange dust; but now, in spring, it was soft and muddy, lush with long green grass everywhere but in the paths.

Derek knew the pattern of each path as he knew the puddles of the road; he could have walked blindfolded along either and still dodged the flat orange patches of mud and trodden accurately on the clumps of grass. But he balanced his way along one edge now on his toes, playing tightrope walker, until he came to the place they had chosen for their camp. It was part of the Ditch wall that was clear of grass. They had begun to dig there, a little, but they had never yet really reached the point of deciding what the camp should be like. So far, it had mostly been talk, and the only thing properly dug, and that very small, was the secret hole.

Derek slipped his hand into the narrow gap cut into the clay wall, masked by a clump of grass. They were still there. He pulled out the rusted, broken spade-stump purloined from his father's trashcan, the blowpipe, and the darts. The spade was pretty useful; it was their only real digging tool, even though it hadn't much of a handle left. There was less use for the blowpipe and darts; none at all really, because even if there had been anything to fire the darts at, the blowpipe would not yet propel them more than a couple of feet. That was his fault. He was the dart-maker; more for the pleasure of the making than for any effect they had. Still you never knew; one day they would work. He fingered a dart now critically. That was a good one: smooth and tough.

Peter and Geoff came whooping toward him along the narrow path. He snatched up the blowpipe hastily and fitted the dart into one end. "Halt! Who goes there!"

"Friends," Geoffrey yelled.

"Prove it."

"Don't be so daft. You know we are."

"All right then, if you can't prove it—" He put the blowpipe to his lips and blew mightily, tightening his lips in the spitting position that his father had taught him as the only way to blow a trumpet or fire a peashooter. He aimed at their feet, but he need hardly have bothered; the dart, as usual, did nothing but curve in a small sad arc as it fell weakly from the end of the pipe. He glared at it, wondering for the hundredth time how natives managed in jungles; and the others jeered.

"You spend ages making those things," Peter said, rubbing the scar on his nose where he had fallen off the back of a truck the year before, "and they never work."

"I don't care. They'll work one day. Hey!" Derek grabbed at Geoffrey, who had retrieved the fallen dart and was trying to take it to pieces.

"All right, all right, keep your shirt on. What you really need is a deadly poison on the point; then it wouldn't have to do more than just scratch someone." He looked around at the mud and long grass. "What's poisonous? Deadly nightshade, laburnum pods . . ."

"Those squishy round white berries at the end of the road."

"Snowballs, they're called."

"It's too early for any of those things anyway," Peter said. He pulled up one of his long gray socks, found it covered in mud, and pushed it down again. "Use dandelion milk—that's just as good. The white stuff that comes out of the stalks."

"That's not poisonous," Geoff said loftily, making his chicken face.

"Bet you it is." Peter pushed his way through the long grass at the bottom of the Ditch, spraying rainwater over his legs and trousers, and pulled a handful of flower stalks from a clump of dandelions. They grew tall there; the picked stalks drooped long, white-green and naked. "Hey," he said to Derek, "rub the darts on them," and together they wetted the sharp wooden points with the white sap that welled in circles from the hollow juicy stems. They took exaggerated care to keep it from their fingers.

"Wouldn't hurt a fly, that stuff," Geoffrey said persistently, with a shade less conviction than before. "You're dippy."

"All right, cleverdick—eat some!" Peter lunged at him with the dandelion stalks; Geoff scrambled just in time up the muddy slope to the side of the Ditch, and they made off in a yelling chase along the muddy path, all the way to where the high wire fence, level with the end of the Robinsons' back garden, cut straight across the Ditch and barred their way. Then slithering down and up again they went, and back along the path on the opposite side. With his pipe and darts stowed safely back in the secret hole, Derek contemplated jumping across to upset Geoffrey in flight, but decided against it. Not fair, really. Too muddy anyway.

"Ah, leave him be, Pete," he called. "It's too wet." Then as they jumped back down to a laughing halt,

"He knows it is poisonous anyway, or he wouldn't have run."

"Well," Geoff said. "Whose idea was it to put stuff on the darts in the first place?"

He was always like that, Derek thought: he could

always twist things around so that even when he was in the wrong, he made it look as though he were in the right. He wouldn't ever be like other people, wouldn't ever admit he could be soft, too. That was the way Geoff was, always wriggling around things. He wasn't sure whether he admired it as persistence or scorned it as cheating.

"Want to dig?" he said at large, fingering the spade.

"No—too sticky," Peter said. "Be like toffee. That's why I didn't bring the boxes up yet."

"What shall we do, then?"

"Plan the camp."

"We're always planning it."

"Not properly. We haven't drawn a plan."

Peter seized a piece of stick from the Ditch bottom and squatted down, making marks on the mud. "Here's the side of the Ditch, see, and there's the hole we dug. And we want the walls to come out here, like this—" The stick, which was frail and rotted, broke as he dug it into the mud.

"That's no good. Why not make proper marks, in the place we're going to do the digging?" said Geoff.

The sense of this was unanswerable; yet Peter, halted in first spate, seemed to be casting about for objections. Derek felt the same reluctance; after all, the planning was fun, the planning was always the best part of anything, to be savored, not to be cut short. He said, "They wouldn't last. The rain would wash them away."

"Mark them with stones," said Geoff, inexorable. "We'll get some from the road. Come on."

He scrambled to the path and made off toward

Everett Avenue, and they followed him more slowly, still reluctant, with a vague sense that the proper order of things was being outraged. Sounds of clattering pots came from Mrs. Robinson's back door as they passed, but they could see no one there. When they caught up with Geoff at the beginning of the Ditch, they found him standing still, gazing across Everett Avenue, at the near end of the White Road. He was watching something with a strange intentness; he looked somehow as if he would have been watching from a secret hiding place if there had been anywhere to hide.

They saw a group of the Children from the White Road crouched together at the end of their territory, bordering on Everett Avenue. Some hidden, intent activity was going on in the middle of the group, like the quivering of a pot of water about to boil. Then suddenly the children jumped to their feet, the group exploded, and they could see one boy standing in the center: a weaselly boy in a dirty gray sweater.

"It's that David Wiggs," Derek said scornfully. Then he stopped.

David Wiggs was holding one arm out, stiffly extended, and jerking it up and down, while the other boys around him capered and laughed. From his hand hung a piece of rope, and at the other end of the rope dangled a struggling black cat, the noose that was around its neck tightening each time David Wiggs's hand jerked. Another boy was poking it in the belly with a piece of stick while it twitched and strangled. It was a small cat. They could hear it making a small hideous yowling sound.

Derek stood gaping, paralyzed, watching someone do

something he thought no one could possibly ever do; he jumped as Peter at his side yelled indignantly, "Stop it!" He felt rather than saw Peter stoop quickly and grab a handful of stones, and then he was doing the same, and both of them were sending a small fusillade of stones toward the group.

A small boy at the edge of the group jumped and squealed, rubbing his arm, and began to cry shrilly; the Children from the White Road scattered, and David Wiggs let go his rope and dropped the cat, which turned a somersault, found its feet, streaked away up the road, and at once disappeared. Then the stones were coming back at them; not from all the group, but from David Wiggs and two of the other larger boys. In the first rush of revenge, they bent down, grabbed, threw; but the rage was not enough to send them rushing into Everett Avenue territory, as it was not enough to make the gang of three carry on their attack now that the wretched anonymous cat had run free.

So the stones and the throwing died away, and most of the White Road children drifted away, back up the road, leaving only the weaselly Wiggs boy and his henchmen yelling insults. In unspoken agreement Derek, Peter, and Geoffrey loftily turned their backs and walked—taking great care, great breathless care not to run—down to Derek's gate.

"That David Wiggs is beastly."

"He's a pig."

"He's a Nazi. And his nose runs."

"I wonder whose cat that is," Peter said, looking worried. He loved all animals, even the evil-smelling chickens his parents kept at the end of their garden.

"Probably a stray," Geoffrey said. "My dad says there are lots more strays about, cats and dogs as well. When people get killed by the bombs, their dogs just run off."

"What do they live on?"

"I dunno. Rats. Mice. Same things wild dogs live on."

"There are wild cats, aren't there?"

"Maybe that cat'll grow up wild and come back and eat David Wiggs."

"Stinky old Wiggs, he'd taste awful."

"Like maggots."

"Like rotten potatoes."

"They only go wild in wild places," Geoffrey said patiently. "On moors and things. That cat'll eat rats and mice in people's back gardens."

"Bet you've never seen a rat," Peter said.

"We caught three mice in traps this winter. My mum says there are rats in the Ditch."

"Go on," said Derek with scorn. Living one house-width away from the Ditch, he felt himself its guardian.

"There are probably. You don't know. Just because you haven't seen any. My mum says we shouldn't go there so much."

"Well, you don't have to," Peter said promptly, "if you want to be Mummy's good boy."

"Shut up."

Peter clicked the latch of the Brands' gate up and down, then pushed it wide. "Hey," he said. "Let's go and see Hughie." Himself an only child, he was fond of Derek's small brother; often, to Derek's gratified astonishment, he would plunge enthusiastically into the middle of any earnest, boring small-child game that might be in progress when he turned up at the house. Geoffrey, walking into the same circumstance, would shortly walk out again; to him Hugh was no more than an uninteresting piece of furniture. In his own family the indulgence due to a youngest child was all his property; he had two sisters much older than himself, large plump, giggling girls who on certain shameful occasions had been heard by Peter and Derek referring to him as "Geoff-geoff."

They clattered up the concrete path and in at the back door. Mrs. Brand was peeling potatoes at the sink.

"Where's Hugh, Mum?"

"Having his nap."

"Oh," Peter said. "Will he be awake soon, Mrs. Brand?"

"Not really, dear. He's only just gone down." Mrs. Brand smiled at him. She liked Pete; all grownups did. Perhaps it was the scar on his nose.

"Oh, well," Derek said. "We'll come back. We'll be in the back field. All right, Mum?"

"All right." She added automatically, "Be careful of the fence."

They filed out again. "See you later, Mrs. Brand," Peter said as he left, and she looked up and smiled again, at his back, with the smile that came usually only for Derek and Hugh.

The three boys trotted in line automatically, back past the air-raid shelter and the vegetable patch. This was the next best place to go, after the Ditch, if the weather was good, though always it had to be at Derek's suggestion, because the back field was his place, his and Hugh's, to be reached only from his garden. They had no idea who owned it. It was simply a field, and dimly they could remember a time when it had been one of several, all golden and scarlet in summer with poppies and wind-rippled wheat. Now, the wheat had gone. The back field was a wilderness, bounded by wire fences, and beyond it was a great patchwork of small allotment gardens where people grew vegetables to help the War Effort. To the right was a line of poplar trees, back boundary of some big unknown house on the main highway. To the left was the continuation of the Ditch, the part that was cut off from the Everett Avenue side by the fence that ran across it. Only the farther side of this part of the Ditch was unfenced, where it opened onto a long field of cabbages that stretched between the allotment gardens and the top half of Everett Avenue all the way to the railroad track.

Peter and Geoff clambered up and over the Brands' garden fence, a foot or two higher than their heads, and dropped, whooping, down into the back field. Derek prowled along the inside looking for his latest discovery; he had found two loose planks only the day before and given them a little—only a little, only a very little—extra loosening to turn them into a workable exit. There they were. He peered at the edges for jutting splinters as he squeezed through.

"Ow!" Too wary of the splinters to remember what was waiting on the other side, within two paces he found himself in a patch of stinging nettles, thick and venomous with the enthusiastic new growth of spring. Geoffrey and Peter joined him, and with cautious viciousness they trod the new stalks down to the ground.

"Did you bust those planks?" Geoff said. "You'll catch it when your dad sees. That's a good way out."

"Look for a dock leaf," Peter said, watching Derek rub his smarting ankles. "There's always one next to the nettles. Here you are." He crushed the broad mottled leaf into a ball, and Derek rubbed it gratefully on his skin. The tingling pain grew less, and the white rash sprang up like a flag.

"Bet that hurts," Geoffrey said.

"Not much."

"Ooh, what a hero."

"Shut up."

"Why should I?"

"Cause I'll shove you in the nettles if you don't, that's why." Derek lunged at him, then relented. "Hey, look for a ball, a yellow one. I lost it last night." He never kept a ball for long. The garden was too small. From the neighboring gardens a ball could—depending on the neighbor's mood—be retrieved, but not from the back field. In summer it would lose itself in the long grass; in spring it would make unerringly for an impenetrable bramble patch. There were several bramble patches, one of them as big as a small house. Derek's year always contained long deprived periods when he owned no ball, and in the summer he would practice bowling with small stunted windfall apples instead. But there were no apples yet on the four trees; only the round flower buds beginning to glimmer red through the new leaves. He thought regretfully of his newest ball; it had lasted since Christmas, until vanishing over the fence the day before in a high golden arc.

"Listen!" Peter straightened up suddenly, with his head tilted to the sky.

They heard a murmur of engines, growing somewhere out of the distance.

"Get down! Over there!"

They ran to the great central bramble patch and with conscious drama flung themselves down in the grass at its edge. The grass was wet. "We'll catch it," Derek thought. The rumbling in the sky grew to a roar, and before long, squinting up into the brightness, they saw the dark shapes of three planes, flying in a tight arrowhead fairly high up. They looked very clear and small in the empty sky.

Peter scrambled to his feet. "That's all right. They're ours."

"Spitfires," Derek said, after an extra moment's careful peering.

Geoffrey said, "I could have told you that from the engines."

"Why didn't you, then?"

"Wanted to see if you knew."

"Go on," Peter said contemptuously.

"I did know," Geoff shouted, his face reddening.

The three Spitfires disappeared past the tall poplar trees at the far end of the back field, and the rumble of their engines went away after them. There was left in the misty spring day no sound but the rustle of the breeze in the poplars, a sound like the breathing of waves against a beach. Shortly their murmur was invaded by the chuffing rattle of a freight train as it crawled into view, its two engines hissing and gasping and belching out black smoke: "Doubleheader," said Derek casually. "Just taken on coal." For a while it stopped and moved and stopped again in despairing jerks, the cars running into one another in a jingling, clanging rat-tat-tat at every stop, until the train picked up speed gradually and heaved its long cargo of canvas-muffled cars steadily, endlessly, out of sight.

"Eighty-five," they chanted. "Eighty-six, eighty-seven, GUARD'S VAN."

"Long one."

"Not so long as that one last week."

"Hundred and two. That was a record."

"There haven't been any other hundreds," Derek reported. His was the only garden with a view of the railway line. "A seventy-fiver yesterday. It might have been a bit longer, but I lost count for a bit because Hugh fell in the mud."

"My uncle drives trains like those," said Peter.

"You told us," Geoffrey said.

Derek said, "I thought we were looking for my ball?"

"Your old ball. Well, which way did it go?"

"Sort of sideways. That way."

"It must be in the big patch, then. We'd never find it in there."

They wandered around the bramble thicket, peering vainly in through the tangled branches and swatting at outflung new shoots that hooked prickles neatly into their jerseyed backs and sleeves.

"Stupid thing," Derek said. "It never even has any blackberries that you can reach. The birds get them all."

He picked a new leaf, flattening its tiny, tender spines

with his thumb; rolled a tight, hard flower bud between his fingers. The thicket stretched far above their heads, almost to the top of the heavy wire fence that ran as a barrier between the back field and the extension of the Ditch, all the way to the allotments. That part of the Ditch was barred from them by fences on three sides. Though it was open to the cabbage field beyond, there was no way of reaching the cabbage field either. You could have gotten there only by going up to the top of Everett Avenue and around through the soldiers' camp (impossible) or by climbing over the back-garden fence of any of the houses farther up. And although their parents knew the people in those houses —everybody knew everybody else on Everett Avenue —they themselves had no friends there. Indeed, there were no children in any of those families to be friends with, only babies, and one small unthinkable girl their own age, with long golden hair, a high whining voice, and a small baby carriage over which she could sometimes be seen leaning in the distance, on the pavement outside her own house, talking to dolls.

So there was no way over, and certainly none through, those back-garden fences.

They were all resting aimlessly against the wire now, staring through. The holes of the mesh were large and diamond-shaped, and the wire was more than strong enough to take their weight if they had tried to climb it. But unhappily, the mesh, though large, was not quite large enough to admit a foot even without its shoe.

"Now that," said Derek, repeating a frequent comment, "would really be the place to build the camp."

"Just down there," said Geoffrey, his nose through the wire. "Close to the brambles. This bit of the Ditch is much nicer than ours."

"Nobody ever throws any rubbish in it either," Derek said.

"They aren't supposed to throw it in the other end."

"They do, though. Sometimes. Those kids."

Geoffrey made a rude noise: a ritual, to be performed at any mention of the Children from the White Road. The ritual had fallen into disuse lately, but it would be back now for a few weeks, after the incident of the cat.

Peter looked along the fence to the far corner of the field. "That's the way your dad goes through to the allotments, isn't it?"

"There's a stile. I'll show you." Derek led the way to the rough wooden plank, set between two crooked posts, that was the only way from the back field to the great patchwork stretch of allotment gardens beyond. His father worked one of the plots on weekends, growing potatoes and beetroot and carrots and long-legged brussels sprouts. Derek had watched him digging there the day before. "Dad brings his spade over the back fence and goes this way, so does Mr. Wishart next door, and Mrs. Hansen's lodger. Everyone else has to go around, though, and come in from the main highway."

"My dad does that," Peter said.

"I didn't know he had an allotment."

"It's right down the other end. He doesn't go there much. He just grows spuds. And we get groundsel from the paths sometimes for the chickens." Peter hoisted himself up on the stile and gazed around.

Derek cleared his throat apologetically. "I'm not supposed to go on the allotments unless I'm helping Dad. He made me promise. He says there's a rule, or something."

"There is. It's a government rule." Peter was still standing up there, looking about him, his bare knees pressed against the top wooden bar of the stile; then he carefully climbed over and dropped down on the other side. "But if we just stay on the edge here, we aren't on anyone's allotment; it's just waste ground. And nobody can see; there's only a few people digging, and they're right over at the other side. Come on. I just want to look at the fence."

Reluctantly, Derek jumped down after him, and Geoffrey followed. Peter moved up a little way from the stile, past the tall post that ended the big wire-mesh fence, until he was facing the cabbage field and the top end of the Ditch. The barrier that kept him from them was the same fence that separated the back field and the allotments, but it was more fearsome here. Though it was made only of four long single wires, instead of mesh, all the way up to the distant railway line, the wire was barbed wire.

"I don't see why we couldn't get through here," Peter said.

"But it's barbed wire. You'd get scratched to bits."

"And then you'd get lockjaw," Geoffrey said with relish. "That's what happens when you get rust in a scratch. Your jaw goes all stiff, and you can't open your mouth, and you can't eat or drink, so you just starve to death."

Peter ignored him. "Look, Derry," he said. "If I

push down the bottom bit of wire, like this, and hold up the top three, then you can squeeze in between them and get through. I won't let it stick in you, honest. Go on, try."

"He's scared," Geoffrey said.

"I am not," said Derek, who was. He looked nervously over his shoulder at the allotments, but saw no change in the few figures bent devotedly over spade or fork; he looked up at the cabbage field and in front of him at the length of the Ditch, but could see nobody there. So he squeezed himself headfirst through the gap that Peter was holding open, caught only the edge of one shoe on the barbed wire, and tumbled down into the long grass on the other side. Then he held the wire in turn, and Peter came after him.

"You coming, Geoff?"

"I'll keep watch," Geoffrey said.

Peter was already in the Ditch, trampling his way through nettles and grass. He clambered down to its lowest point, facing a steep embankment over which a few brambles reached feeble arms in escape from the back field thicket held back by the tall mesh fence. He ducked down, so that they could see only a glimpse of his fair head among the leaves and the mounds of clay, and then bounced up again, grinning with delight.

"Hey, this is smashing. Come and see. We've got to build the camp here."

As Derek slithered down, half the world disappeared. The weed-feathered sides of the Ditch cut him off from Geoffrey, the cabbages, the surrounding fences and houses; and there was left only the tall side fence of the

back field, with that gigantic sinister blackberry bush that seemed from here to be trying to push it down. There was a glimpse of the similar fence that crossed the Ditch between the Robinsons' and the Twyfords' gardens, cutting off their own usual road-linked world; and nothing else but the sky. He stared happily about him at the orange-red earth and the lush grass and the rank clumps of weed.

Peter punched his arm lightly. "Like it?"

"It's perfect. Nobody would ever find it here. We could build a really good one and keep all sorts of things."

"The way this hump here goes, look, we could just hollow out a bit of the back wall and put a roof across from it to the hump, and it would be like a room. Like our Morrison, almost."

"Like the way the sandbags are around the guns up the road."

"We could even get some sandbags."

"Um."

They pondered this for a moment. Somehow sandbags would not be right for their own camp. It was a timeless fortification, theirs; it grew in their minds out of a vague mixture of Iron Age earthworks and Saxon forts. They had known about such things for as long as they could remember, and not from books or school. The leavings of the ancient peoples were all around them in the valley of the Thames and the Chiltern Hills. Regularly they saw them, passed them, walked over them: the once-besieged fortresses, ten centuries old, which lay gentle now beneath soft. sloping grassy mounds.

"Not sandbags," Derek said.

"No. But we could put a roof. The boxes would be good for that."

"Have to do the digging first. Let's get the spade from the old camp."

"Hey!" A plaintive yell came faintly down from the other side of the fence. Derek started, feeling guilty. He had completely forgotten about Geoffrey, keeping watch.

"That Geoff," said Peter.

"Careful. He might have seen someone."

They wriggled along the bottom of the Ditch, around the big clay hummock, and peered carefully up through the grass.

Geoffrey called, "You think you're so good at stalking. I can see you plain as anything. Lucky for you I'm not Mr. Everett."

Peter stood up. "You've never seen Mr. Everett."

"Nor have you. Come on, you've been down there for ages."

Derek heaved himself up, picking last year's burrs off his sweater. "Come and look, Geoff. It's just the right place for the camp."

"It's a moldy place," Geoffrey said peevishly. "How can we come and go through that stupid barbed-wire fence? And I'm fed up with standing here keeping lookout. There isn't even anywhere for me to hide if anyone comes."

"Nobody asked you to keep lookout," Peter said coolly. Then he relented and gave Geoff his sudden crooked grin. "Come on, hold the wire for me. We have to go and get the spade and everything from the old camp and bring them here to start digging. It really is a super place; wait till you see. There's loads of space to make storage holes. We can make a special hidden one to take birds' eggs."

This was a deliberate peace offering; neither he nor Derek approved of collecting birds' eggs, regarding it as a particularly shameful kind of robbery. But Geoffrey, firmly explaining that he did no harm by taking only one egg from each nest, did collect them, and messily blow them, and keep them labeled in boxes in his room. When they had first thought of building the camp in their usual section of the Ditch, he had greeted the thought of it delightedly as a way station for newly taken eggs.

"So long as you don't touch our robin," Derek said. A robin had nested two years running in a bush in the Brands' front garden; this was the first year they had let Geoff see the tiny pale blue eggs.

"I got a robin egg ages ago," Geoffrey said loftily. But he was mollified. "Well, let me come through and see, then, if it's so marvelous."

"Come and get our things first," Peter said. He scrambled through the fence, casually ripping out a thread from his sleeve as it caught on the sharp hooked wire. "Why'n't you stay here, Derry, and keep an eye on it? We shan't be a minute. If we see your mum, I'll tell her we're just playing in the back field."

"All right. Better tell her I'll be in soon. And mind you get my blowpipe and darts."

He called after them, "Be careful with the darts. There's seven of them."

From the stile, Geoffrey called over his shoulder, "They don't *work.*"

"We'll be careful," Peter said.

Derek clambered down again into the Ditch as they disappeared toward his back garden. A lone cabbage white butterfly flittered around his head, lighted briefly on a patch of bare clay, and meandered off again. He swiped at it absently, out of habit. Down at the bottom, he pulled a few clumps of weeds from the area that would be the floor of the camp, and stamped the ground down as flat as he could make it. Really, it would be a wonderful secret place. A real camp, this time.

He heard the sound of engines, crouched, looked up. The three Spitfires were coming back; farther away this time and more strung out. He thought: "I'm going to be a pilot one day. Or no, what I really want is to be a sailor, in a destroyer, like Commander Hansen down the road. Or perhaps I'll be a soldier, like Daddy was in the last war. With a gun."

He thought about the gun. His father was a sergeant now in the local Home Guard; his newly acquired steel helmet, which he called a tin hat, hung in the hall on the hatstand, and the heavy service rifle stood on its butt in the umbrella stand beneath it. The strictest rule in the house was that nobody should ever, on any account, touch John Brand's gun. Derek had touched it only once, on the day it first appeared, when his father had ceremonially put the tin hat on his head and the rifle in his hands. They had both weighed several tons. The helmet had been so heavy that Derek's chin had bent down to his chest for the second that John Brand had let the padded metal rest on his head; and the rifle so heavy that even with both hands and all his strength he had been able to lift it for an instant only an inch or two from the floor. And that had been that, and he had never touched the gun again.

The sun was warm. A large sleepy bumblebee wandered past his head. He forgot about the gun.

Then Peter and Geoffrey leaped down into the Ditch, whooping, Geoff carrying the spade and Peter carefully cradling the blowpipe and darts without one dart tip so much as bruised; and they set to digging out the first outline of their camp. They dug for a long while, taking turns with the rusty spade head, and by the time they had to stop for dinner, at Mrs. Brand's distant call from the back garden, the camp was well enough begun to be fitted with its roof.

The sky was clear all day, and still only a few chunky clouds had drifted across it by the time they went to bed. Before his mother pulled the blackout curtains carefully over the windows in the chilly, darkening room, Derek could see the moon sailing tranquilly in and out of the clouds: gradually drifting sideways, moving in an endless flowing motion, and yet hanging always still. Then the shiny black cotton of the curtain blotted everything out, and it was dark.

"There won't be a raid tonight, will there, Mum?"

"Well, darling," she said gently, "I hope there won't."

"There's lots of cloud to cover the moon."

"That's right. Let's hope they stay at home."

"Be awful if they bombed our camp," he said sleepily. "It's smashing. We're going to put a roof on it and camouflage it with grass."

"Remember you promised me there wouldn't be any tunneling," Mrs. Brand said. "That's dangerous."

Derek yawned. "Just walls. And a sort of dent." He had been so full of the thought of the camp that he had had to talk about it; but he had still kept it secret—he hadn't said where it was.

"Good night, Mum."

She kissed him. "Don't forget your prayers. Good night, my love."

Sleepily he murmured the Lord's Prayer to himself and added the usual bit about blessing Daddy and Mum and Hughie.

Hugh coughed, across the room in his cot. There was a muffled sound through the wall, like a shifting chair, from the Robinsons' house next door. Derek snuggled down under his quilt and felt earth still gritty under one of his fingernails.

Please God look after the camp, he added. It sounded a bit odd, somehow, but he didn't think there was anything wrong about it.

Hugh coughed again, twice; stirred, moaned, turned over. "Good night, Derry."

"Good night. Sleep well."

" 'n' you."

And please God don't let there be a raid tonight.

But it was the sirens that woke him. They were all going at once: two of them somewhere farther off, well started on their long-drawn-out, eerie rising and falling note; and then breaking into it suddenly, loud and harsh, their own local siren in the village, curving up out of nowhere in that first throat-catching whine that was the most chilling sound of any except the very last, the long, long, long dying-down wail that was the worst of all. But before the last wail came, they were all on their way out to the air-raid shelter, Derek with boots and two sweaters over his pajamas, and a coat over those; Hugh lying in a bundle of blankets in his father's arms. The night was very cold, and the moon had gone. The guns were already thumping somewhere close by, and planes were rumbling high overhead. As they hurried across the lawn, there was the night-breaking crash of a bomb, and the earth shook.

"Big ones," John Brand said.

Mrs. Brand went quickly down the earthen steps behind the sandbag wall at the shelter's entrance, and he handed Hugh to her and turned to lift Derek down. The noise grew; planes were flying closer, lower, and the world exploded as the guns went into action at the end of the road. "Thunk . . . thunk . . . thuunk-thunk . . ."

Derek gazed upward, openmouthed, as light streaked across the sky and great sudden stars burst; the long white arms of the searchlights were groping to and fro in the black sky from those unknown places across the railway where they always sprang up at night, and one of them seemed to have gone mad. It was darting and weaving like a clumsy giant, and he saw the silhouette of a plane in its white light, a plane flying low, and he thought he could even see the crosses on its wings as

another engine screamed and a Spitfire—he could see the pointed nose—came diving toward it through the beam.

"Derek!" John Brand yelled.

The sky flashed, and somewhere another of the great bombs burst. Derek went to his father, but his head was still back as he moved, the searchlight hypnotically holding his eyes. That plane was out of the light; you could hear it diving, shrieking; it was coming nearer, nearer—

"Get down," John Brand shouted furiously, and grabbed him and pushed him so roughly inside the shelter door that Derek lurched and fell over his mother's knees where she sat on one of the bunks. His father ducked down after him, and the plane roared as it dived over the road, and there was a rapid, horrible clatter sweeping across the world with it at the peak of the noise. The guns everywhere were hammering the sky in an uneven thunder, and close together there were several great blasting crashes as more bombs fell.

John Brand pulled the wooden cover over the shelter entrance and tugged down the curtain that hung behind it, and Mrs. Brand lit a candle that stood waiting in a wax-scarred saucer on the shelf nailed to the corrugated metal wall. Outside, the bumps and bangs went on. Derek sat down suddenly on the bottom bunk and burst into tears.

His father sat down beside him and held him tightly. "I'm sorry, Derry. Are you all right?"

Miserably Derek nodded, unable to speak for the sobs that were sending his chest up into his throat. He pressed his head hard into his father's arm and clutched at his hand.

"I didn't mean to be rough," John Brand said. "But you mustn't ever be outside when a raid's going on. Never. Never. You know the rules. You must always get into a shelter as quickly as you possibly can. Or if there isn't a shelter, then into a ditch, or under a tree, or anywhere close to the ground. You aren't really old enough to be frightened, and because you aren't, you just must remember the rules. Understand?"

Swallowing, choking, Derek nodded again. He said, through gulps, "I'm sorry."

His father's arm around him was like an iron bar. He said softly, "We don't want to lose you."

Derek looked up, blinking in the wavering yellow light of the candle, and saw Hugh watching him from wide dark eyes in the opposite bunk, and his mother sitting there silent beside him, holding his hand. She gave him a small encouraging smile, and he saw that her face was wet. "Oh, Mum," he said unsteadily, nearly beginning again, and lurched across the shelter. "I'm sorry, Mum."

She hugged him and wiped his face. "There now," she said. "But you must remember what Daddy said. Always."

"We always get down somewhere if we hear planes when we're out," Derek said. "Even if the warning hasn't gone. Until we can see whether they're ours."

"That's very good," his mother said. "Now you get up into your bunk, and I'll tuck the blanket around you. We may be here for a while tonight. You close your eyes and try to get some rest. You, too, Hughie, lie down now and go to sleep."

There was another great thump outside, and the earth gently shook. Opening his eyes, Derek saw from his bunk the jerk of the candle flame and the quiver in the thin dark line of greasy smoke that rose from it to the low curved metal roof.

"Don't worry," his father said, watching him. "They're going away. Our battery has stopped firing. It won't be too long now."

Derek lay there, pressing his boots against the end of the bunk; feeling the blanket rough against his chin; smelling the shelter smell of dank earth and candle grease. He thought sleepily, "But I'm not worried." He had never been frightened by the bombs. The raids were always an excitement, though a mixed excitement because he knew going down to the shelter made Hugh's cough worse. That was the only reason for not wanting a raid: that and the camp. Like anybody else, he knew what it was like to be scared by things like the snapping of a large dog, by bigger boys chasing him at school, by being alone in the dark. But the guns and the bombs and the swooping planes, they were different. Nothing about them had ever really bothered him before—not, at any rate, until that fierce moment this evening, with the strange urgent note in his father's voice and the violence with which he had pulled him down. Derek gulped again at the thought of it. That had scared him all right. It was so totally out of character in his gentle father; he had never seen anything like it before. "I won't ever hang about again when we're coming down here," he thought earnestly; "I'll get in as quick as ever I can."

The thumping of the guns grew more muffled; merged into a familiar, almost comforting background, with Hugh's occasional cough and his parents' intermittent soft murmuring below. Derek drifted into sleep, thinking: "I hope the camp's all right. I hope they didn't get the camp."

4

Monday

The camp was intact. They were working on it again by the time the next morning was halfway through. The three of them had walked together to school as they always did: up Everett Avenue, across the main highway, and along the three side streets lined with gigantic metal objects like candlesticks that put up the smokescreen to protect the housing estate in a raid. As they turned the corner toward the school, they could see the crowd that told them something was wrong, and they broke into a run, with Peter in front as he always was sooner or later. Within moments they were in the thick of the crowd and gazing down at the huge gaping hole in the road outside the gates of the school.

Derek stood staring, mesmerized. He had seen bomb craters before, but they had always been in fields. A hole in a field, even a huge hole, was not the same as a hole in a road; this was more violent, somehow, with yards and yards of road and pavement simply gone, vanished, and the road surface and stones and gravel and clay and broken pipes left naked in layers, as if by a vast jagged slice taken from a gigantic cake. When he looked around again, he saw that there was another crater close by, where the garden of the house next door to the school had been, and that there was not much house left either, but only a heap of rubble and one lonely wall.

"The old lady was in there." Peter was back at his side, wide-eyed from gathering reports. "The bomb fell right on the house, and she got killed. There was a whole stack of bombs, bong, bong, bong. They say he must have been just getting rid of them, Jerry that is, to get away from the fighters quicker. Nobody else got killed. They say he wasn't aiming at anything. I dunno though; I bet he was aiming at the school. I bet he was trying to hit us."

"But it was the middle of the night," Derek said.

"Well, maybe he thought it was a boarding school." Peter was not to be put off. "Then he could have got hundreds of us with one bomb."

"And all he got was old Mrs. Jenkins." Derek tried to think about old Mrs. Jenkins, who had been a familiar figure beaming out at all of them every morning and every afternoon, even though a few incorrigibles picked all her reachable roses and wrote rude words on her fence; and he found that he could not remember a line of her face, but only her cracked voice calling over the frosted path, one winter's day, "Good morning, boys."

"I was looking for shrapnel," Peter said. "But it's

all gone. And you can't get down into the crater because they've got that rope around it. What a swizz."

"I found a bit in the garden this morning," Derek said.

"Did you really? Let's have a look."

Derek reached carefully into his pocket and unwrapped the small jagged piece of metal from his handkerchief. He had found it quite by accident when kicking a pebble along the front garden path, and felt as though he had come across the Koh-i-noor diamond. Each of the boys had a handful of pieces of shrapnel

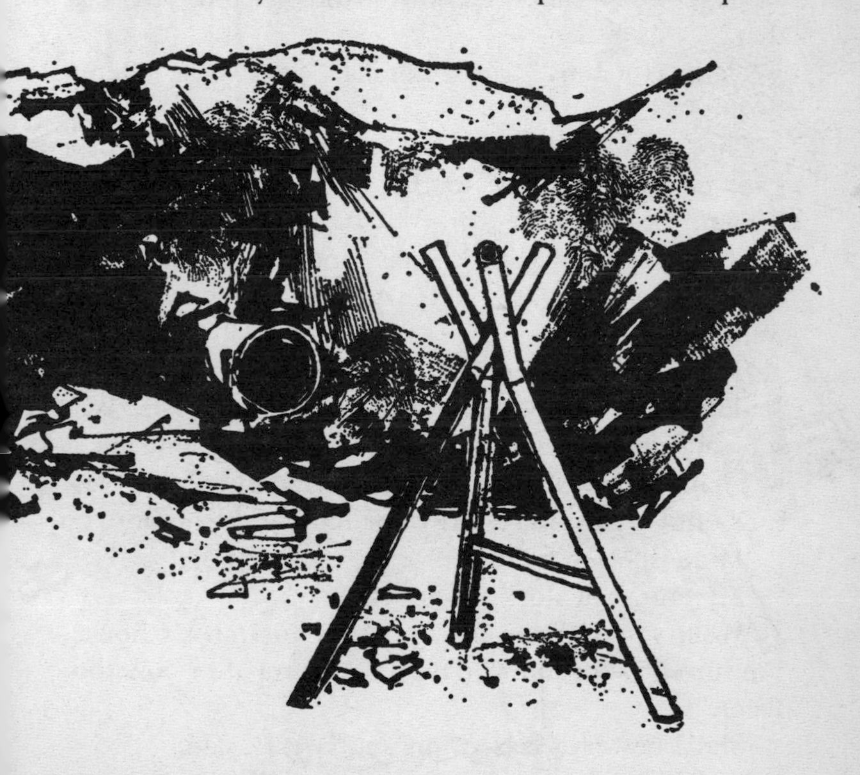

recovered from bomb craters or exploded shells, but they were hard to come by; too many other people had generally gotten there first.

"That's a smashing bit," Peter said generously. "Must be from a shell. That raid went on for ages."

"Um," Derek said. Usually they went over their memories of night raids in lurid and exaggerated detail, but he found himself curiously reluctant this time. He said offhandedly, "They were machine-gunning the road."

"Yes," Peter said. "I know." And he, too, left it at that.

"Peter Hutchins," said a familiar, clear voice. "Derek Brand."

They turned and saw Mrs. Wilson stepping out of a knot of teachers close to the school gate. "Morning, ma'am," they said.

"That *crater,* ma'am," Peter said. "Did you know old Mrs. Jenkins got killed? Did they hit the school as well?"

"It was very sudden, and we must be glad poor Mrs. Jenkins didn't know what was happening," Mrs. Wilson said gently. "And no, the school wasn't hit, but it was damaged by the blast, and we shan't be having lessons until Wednesday. Are your mothers at home?"

"Mine is," Derek said.

"My mum's at work," Peter said.

"Well, you'd better both go back to Derek's house. I'm sure Mrs. Brand won't mind looking after you, too, Peter."

"She'd be very pleased, ma'am," Derek said.

Mrs. Wilson's mouth twitched, and she patted him

on the shoulder. They liked Mrs. Wilson. She was quite old, even older than their mothers, and she yelled at you and sometimes threw chalk if you made a noise in class, but she was all right, Mrs. Wilson was. They liked her. Neither of them could have explained why.

Mrs. Wilson said, "Is Geoffrey Young with you?"

Peter looked at the crowd. "He's in there somewhere."

"His mum's at home," Derek said.

"All right. I'll see him if you don't. But you have a look for him now, and all three of you go along home. There's nothing to see here now. And remember school starts again as usual the day after tomorrow. You don't get any more extra holiday than that, even if Jerry tried to get you one."

They laughed, said "Thank you, ma'am; good-by, ma'am," found Geoffrey, and ran home. They talked about the stick of bombs all the way. To have a bomb just miss the school, now that was something. "Just suppose it had been in the daytime," they said to one another with relish. "Just suppose we'd all been there." And at no point did Derek link the possibility with the events and emotions and memories of the night before. They were hardly even memories now, or would not be until the dark came down again and the air-raid warning came howling out.

The camp was developing quickly. They carved out a hole in one side and fitted one of Peter's packing cases in to act as a cupboard; they opened the second box out to lie flat, or flattish, for a roof, banged all the protruding nails flat with a stone, dug out a deep slit in the orange clay, and fitted it in. This took a long time, not least because only two of them were ever working at once. They took turns keeping watch on the other side of the fence, safe in the back field, just in case someone—anyone—might pass and see what they were doing and tell them they shouldn't be doing it.

When the roof, or part roof, was on, they stood back and surveyed the camp. It was a V-shaped room now, with two bare earth walls formed by the side and end of the Ditch. Peter and Derek packed a thin layer of earth carefully over the roof, stuffing handfuls of grass into any slits where it dribbled through, and made complicated and not very effective attempts to plant tufts of growing grass on top of it. "Camouflage," Peter said. "Like those pictures of soldiers with branches stuck onto their tin hats."

"Like the way they paint everything brown and green—aircraft hangers and the factory chimneys on the estate."

"What about the edge of the roof?" demanded Geoffrey, arriving with a critical eye from his tour on watch.

"You can't cover that. The earth just drops off."

"Well, it sticks out like anything. It's all white. You can see it miles away."

"We can dirty it." Peter rubbed a damp handful of clay along the bright edge. "And we can dig up some little bushes or something and plant them in front here, and they'll grow up and hide the whole thing. And we'll have a wall sticking out half the way across, so the entrance'll be between that and the other side of the Ditch."

"With gaps on the top of it to fire over," Derek said. "Like a castle."

"Battlements," said Geoffrey.

"Battlements," Peter said thoughtfully. But nobody said anything about a battle.

They all went home to dinner. Peter's mother was at home after all; they had called in at his house on the way, to collect their packing cases, and found her. The factory where she worked had been bombed in the raid the night before. They had asked whether anyone had been killed, and she had told them abruptly to go away and play.

Geoffrey came knocking at the back door in the afternoon. "Can Derry come out, Mrs. Brand?"

Derek came out. It was a gray day, but no raid had arrived yet; the air and the breeze were still dry. "Where's Pete?" he said.

"I don't know. He wasn't there. Nobody was. I suppose his mum took him shopping." Geoffrey brought out the idea with distaste and some scorn. To each of them a shopping trip was a shameful occupation, but he was the only one who could afford to say so. The one advantage of having two elder sisters was their endless willingness to trot off, even with no clothing coupons in their pockets, to inspect shop windows in the town to which the buses went.

"Swizz," Derek said. In silence, they made for the camp. He never felt quite at his ease when he was alone with Geoffrey; somehow it was difficult to know what to talk about. Pete and he could be alone for hours and neither really consciously notice that the other was there; their talking was a thinking aloud. But Geoffrey was peculiar. You were always aware, in some way, that you didn't know what was going on inside his head, and sometimes he would suddenly come out with some remark that made it clear he thought there was something sinister or discreditable going on inside yours. And it was always at a time when you were just thinking about the weather or the shape of a tree or nothing at all.

He dug away at the side and bottom of the Ditch, building up the new wall; pausing now and then to puff and to scrape off chunks of clinging earth from the small, stubby, impractical spade. Geoff worked fussily at the end of the wooden roof, coating small precise areas so that eventually they darkened to the color of the Ditch itself. It was, Derek had to admit to himself, far more effective than Peter's sweeping attempt of the morning. The day was still cool and gray, but the two of them were warm with work, saying little, except when one would stop, stand critically back, and demad the other's approval of what he had done.

Then there was a whoop and a sudden rustling in the grass, and Derek dropped the spade and Geoff stumbled and bumped his nose on the roof, and Peter rose out of nowhere and jumped over the humped end of the Ditch to come bouncing down between them.

"Caught you! I'm a scout party from the gun camp. What do you kids think you're up to, eh?"

"Aren't you clever," said Geoffrey resentfully, rubbing his nose.

Derek grinned. "Where've you been?"

"You're lousy lookouts," Peter said. "I mean I was right on top of you, I could see everything you were doing, and you didn't even notice I was there. I might have been anybody." He looked at the wall and the dark-edged roof. "Hey, that's good. That looks super."

Derek said, pleased, "Well, you weren't anybody, were you?"

"You made enough row to bring everybody after you," Geoff said. He stood up, dabbing at his nose for signs of blood but finding none; and then he crouched suddenly, and his voice dropped to a hiss. "There *is* someone—get down—there's somebody on the allotments over the other side of the fence. You daft thing, Pete, he must have heard you."

Peter remained where he was. "That's all right," he said cheerfully. "I brought him with me."

"But the camp's secret," Derek said.

"That's Tom Hicks," Peter said. "You know Tommy Hicks. From the top of the road."

Derek peered suspiciously at the back of the tall figure standing a few yards away in the allotment field. "Yuh, that big boy, I remember him. Haven't seen him for ages, though."

"He's at home for a bit. I saw him at his house after dinner; I had to go up with my mum to deliver something or other, and she wanted me to see his mum. He's been working away from home somewhere, in a factory I think." Peter took breath for his announcement. "He's going into the Merchant Navy next month."

"Coo," they said. There were few soldiers, sailors, or airmen on Everett Avenue, and fewer contacts with them; mostly there were only parents who were too old for the war and children who were too young. One or two husbands and elder sons had disappeared, like Commander Hansen and the Jones boy from the house opposite Geoffrey's, but they were simply absences.

Nobody had seen them yet since they went; they had never been home on leave. Tommy Hicks was going to join them, Tommy Hicks was visible, so Tommy Hicks had glamour and all the aura of mysterious bravery that went with the endless war.

"Hey, Tom," Peter called confidently. "Come over and see our camp."

Derek and Geoffrey watched shyly as the bigger boy, big as an adult, pushed down on the top strand of the barbed wire and cocked first one leg and then the other over it, neat as could be, without much effort at all. "*That* fence wouldn't keep many Jerries out," Derek thought with something like shame. "It wouldn't keep anyone out much except little kids. After all, it doesn't even keep us out, even if we can't get over it as easily as him."

Tom Hicks stood smiling down at them. "Hallo there," he said. "You're Derry Brand and Geoff Young, aren't you? I remember you. You've grown up a bit though, I must say." He was tall, broad-shouldered, wearing a roll-neck sweater, with patched gray trousers tucked into rubber boots that would each have held both Derek's feet put end to end. He looked as if he were a sailor already.

"Are you really going in the Merchant Navy?" Derek said.

"Three weeks yesterday," Tom Hicks said. "Report for training the third of May."

"Gosh," Derek said.

Geoffrey said, "My uncle's on a destroyer."

"Which one?" Tommy squatted down companionably on his heels.

"H.M.S. *Hood.*"

He nodded gravely. "That's a good ship."

Geoffrey glanced triumphantly at the others and appeared to swell.

Derek said, "What's the difference between the Merchant Navy and the navy?"

"The *Royal* Navy," Geoffrey said reprovingly.

"Easier to get sunk in the merchant ships," Tommy Hicks said, hugely cool and casual. "Fewer guns. But you can join up younger." He added, pulling at a blade of grass, "My cousin was torpedoed in one last month. Went down in the North Atlantic. They didn't save anybody."

"Gosh," Peter said. "I didn't know that. That's awful."

"There's a war on," Tom said lightly. He eased himself up to his feet again and looked around. "That's a good camp you've got here."

"We've only just started it really."

"We put a bit of a roof on here, see, and camouflaged it." Derek looked at him calculatingly. "I expect you're a bit too big to go inside."

"I expect I am."

"There's going to be a wall over here."

"And a special entrance."

"And we're going to plant a bush or a tree or something to grow over and hide it."

"Use a bit of the bramble bush," Tom said. "That transplants easy. And it'd be just like barbed wire."

They looked at him with respect. "That's a super idea."

"Don't mention it," Tom said. "I can see you've

really been working hard. Stick at it. You never know when it'll come in handy."

"You won't tell anyone about it, will you?" Geoff said.

Peter said indignantly, "Course he won't."

"Course I won't," Tom said.

"How old do you have to be to join the Merchant Navy?" Derek said.

"Sixteen," said Tom. "You'll have to wait a bit."

"Yes. I was planning on flying a Spitfire, actually, but you have to be seventeen to get in the RAF."

"I must go," Tom said. "Tell your mum I was careful climbing over your back fence, Derek."

"Did you see her?"

"She said she didn't mind," Peter said. "We went calling for you first."

"I think your camp's jolly good," Tom said. "Can I come and see it when it's finished?"

"Course you can."

They leaped behind and around him up the end of the Ditch along to the fence. "Hey, stop," said Geoffrey. "Look at that."

They paused and saw a glint of metal in the long grass beside the fence; it was a square closed can, a toffee can, with a pattern of flowers around its printed label. They never saw that sort of can in the shops now. Derek's mother had one from before the war; she kept buttons in it, and its flowered sides were dented and the colors dulled. This one looked brand new. Peter bent down to part the grass.

"Don't touch it!" Geoff yelped. "It might be a

bomb. My dad says Jerry drops things like that so that kids will pick them up and get blown to bits."

Instinctively they all moved back—all except Tom. He stood where he was, looking down at the can, frowning a little.

"Funny we haven't noticed it before," Peter said. He stepped forward again.

"You stay there," Tom said.

"We didn't notice it because it wasn't there," Geoff said. "I bet they dropped it in the raid last night."

It was a trigger: for a dreadfully vivid, unexpected moment Derek was back at the mouth of the shelter, in the crashing, flashing darkness; seeing his father's twisted, shouting face, feeling himself flung backward down the steps, hearing the roar of the low-swooping plane and the rattle of the guns. Sleep had pushed the memory so comfortably deep in his mind that for a moment he could not cope with its engulfing reappearance. He looked at the can and flinched, and knew nothing in the world would have induced him to pick it up.

"And if it's not a bomb and it's got real toffees in it," Geoff said, "then they'll be poisoned, because they try to get kids that way, too. But I bet it is a bomb."

"Go on," Peter said automatically, but there was doubt in his voice.

They all looked fearfully at Tom. He stood there rubbing one boot slowly against the other, and ran a hand thoughtfully through his hair. It was unusual hair: wiry and thick, and very curly, and a dark reddish brown like a new chestnut.

He said, "Bombs go off all sort of ways. Either on impact, when they hit the ground, or when they get near water. There's a puddle over there, so I suppose this doesn't mind water. Or sometimes they have a timing device, and you can usually hear that ticking. Or they go off when they get near metal."

"The spade," Derek said nervously, and looked around; but it was yards away.

Tom bent down close to the can. "No ticking," he said. "If it is a bomb, it's probably booby-trapped, so it would go off when someone opened the lid." He looked across at them. "Here," he said, "you kids get down in the Ditch. Go on. Duck right down."

"You're not going to open it?" Peter said, and his voice cracked into a squeak.

"No, I'm not, I'm not daft. But we can't just leave it lying here. And there's no point getting a bomb disposal squad all this way just to look at a tin—anyway, they're all just blokes like you and me. Well," he said, "like me anyway. Go on, duck down there."

They slithered down over the hummock and peeped across it through the grass. Tommy Hicks bent down slowly and picked up the can, very carefully, keeping it the same way up as it had been lying; and he leaned back and brought his arm back like an outfielder throwing a cricket ball a long way to the wicket, and he hurled the can far up into the empty cabbage field. Watching through the grass, they saw it curve, spinning up against the gray sky and lazily down. Derek could feel the blood thumping in his throat. The can landed and bounced once, and they heard a very faint distant rattle, and that was all.

Everything was very quiet. They drew breath again. Tom had crouched; he straightened and laughed. "False alarm," he said. "No bomb."

"Perhaps it was a dud."

"Perhaps it was a poisoned candy thing after all. And they'll all have spilled out, and someone might eat them."

"No. It wasn't heavy. It must have been an empty tin." Tom laughed again. "Be seeing you," he said, and he stepped straight-legged over the barbed wire, and then over the stile, and disappeared across the back field and the Brands' fence. He turned once and waved. They stood there watching him, reverently.

"The way he chucked that thing," Peter said. "Just picked it up and chucked it."

"I wouldn't have touched it for anything," Derek said.

Geoffrey said, like an old man passing judgment, "He's got guts."

They went back to the building of the camp, rapidly, busily, as if it were an act of tribute.

They worked on the camp for the rest of that day, and for most of the next day, too, their extra holiday given them by the bombing of the school. Mrs. Hutchins went back to work that second day because factories were repaired more quickly than schools, and Peter had his dinner with Derek and Hugh. They ate big floury canned peas, and yesterday's boiled potatoes fried up, and fat sausages that split open all the way down their length almost as soon as they were put in the frying pan, so that the split insides were fried as brown as the skins. Hugh ate very little except mashed-up peas, but then Hugh was only just three years old and never did eat much of anything. Derek liked his sausages that way, but Mrs. Brand sighed over them as she always did.

"Full of bread," she said.

"But there isn't any bread inside, Mum. Just sausage."

"That's not the way sausages used to be," she said. Their parents were always saying things like this. Derek and Peter assumed it to be a natural consequence of growing up. All adults seemed to think there was something peculiar about the world, something to be apologized for. Yet everything was just the same as it had always been. They realized, vaguely, that there had been a time when the raids had not come every night, but that was very dim and a million years ago. It didn't seem to them that the things they ate were any different from the way they had always been. Food was food, after all, and there was always plenty of it. And a great deal nicer at home than it generally was at school. The awfulness of school dinners, the gristly stew and the watery cabbage, was the only mealtime topic about which they ever felt any emotion at all.

Nevertheless, they were back eating their school dinners the next day. The rubble that had been old Mrs. Jenkins's house was still untouched, and the bomb crater was still there in the middle of the road, huger than ever but firmly fenced off with trestles and ropes and red flags that were really pieces of rag knotted to the ropes. Teachers and sometimes a policeman were there keeping watch at the beginning and end of school, and at playtimes and dinnertime, but even so, you could get close enough to see that there was no remaining scrap of shrapnel to be had and that the big pipes in the bottom of the crater had been mended.

Most of the houses on the other side of the road had paper or boards over their windows where the blast had shattered the glass, and one of them had a large chunk of the old road surface lying half across its front-door step. The small boy who lived there was now a playground hero and could be seen every day, before and after school, escorting small troops of listeners across the road into his now fenceless front garden for a close look at the piece of road and a short lurid lecture about what would have happened to his family if it had skated its way a few feet farther on.

His fame lasted for about a week. After that the bomb crater was filled in, and the few remaining jagged pieces of wall from the Jenkins house were pulled down. And the memory of the near miss was eclipsed by a daylight raid that kept the entire school in the air-raid shelters for an hour and a half and produced no bombs, no gunfire, and no sound even of a single plane, but used up half a jar of the headmistress's carefully hoarded shelter-time candy. And the small boy who had been famous was knocked down in the playground by the mean-minded gang of the school bully, just like anyone else, and skinned his knee.

5

Saturday

The sirens had wailed every night of that week, and every night had brought another blurred memory of a stumbling blanket-wrapped walk into the garden; of the shelter smell and the flickering flame of the candle and the thump-thump of the guns.

But the next weekend, Derek and Peter and Geoffrey finished their camp. It was only after they had finished and sat down in it for the first time that they noticed the chill that was in the wind blowing through the gray day; in their hours as preoccupied moles, their business had kept them warm. They looked proudly about them. After some careful hollowing of its sides, the little two-walled, timber-roofed room was big enough now to contain all three of them if they squatted close; they could even sit on its floor, which was covered with newspapers from the wastepaper sack in Derek's garage and was, at least until the next rain fell, not damp. Sitting there, out of the breeze, they could see only the sides of the Ditch and the cloud's and the top—duly battlemented—of the earthen half-wall they had built across the Ditch as a barricade. The box cupboard in the side of the miniature room contained, in neat, proud order, Derek's darts and blowpipe, a flimsy cardboard box holding three of Geoff's birds' eggs, and Peter's six-shooter, which was the most prized and realistic weapon any of them possessed. Two of the eggs that Geoffrey had put there were from a starling's nest and not very special. (Starlings, according to Geoff, were as big and as common a pest as dandelions.) But the third was his only blackbird's egg and therefore had value. Peter's gun had so much value that he was still in two minds whether to leave it in the camp at all. He turned now and picked it up. It was a splendid long-barreled metal gun, friendly to the hand, of a kind that nobody could ever find in a shop now; such things had vanished when the war began, and all money and metal went toward real guns.

"I don't think I ought to leave it," he said.

Geoffrey said reproachfully, "My blackbird's egg is here. And Derry's blowpipe."

"But you could get another egg. And Derry could make another blowpipe."

"But that's not fair. We said we'd all leave something."

"Pete could leave something else," Derek said. "The gun might get rusty. You know how it looked the time we left it in his garden all night."

Geoff said obstinately, "He could wrap it in newspaper. That would keep the damp out."

"Not if it rained. The paper would get sopping."

"No it wouldn't. Not in the secret cupboard. The rain wouldn't get in there."

"You don't know. It hasn't rained yet since we built it. The water might come pouring through."

"Well, it's not fair," Geoffrey said. "If Pete doesn't leave his gun here, I'm taking my blackbird's egg home."

"You are mean," Derek said, suddenly furious. "You're spoiling everything. You always do. You like spoiling things."

Geoffrey turned crimson. He stood up. "All right," he said tremulously, and he bent and took the box with the eggs inside and cradled it under one arm. "You're always on Pete's side. Everything's always my fault. Well, you can keep your stupid camp. I'm going home."

"Oh, come on, Geoff." Peter scrambled up and dabbed awkwardly at his shoulder. "Come on. Put the eggs back. I'll leave my gun here, too. He's quite right," he said sideways to Derek. "It wouldn't be fair if I didn't."

Geoffrey paused and kicked at the side of the Ditch.

"Come on," Peter said again.

"Well," Geoff said, and he sniffed. "Well, Derry's got to say he's sorry."

"What for?" Derek said indignantly.

"For saying beastly things, that's what."

"I only said—" Derek stopped. Peter's heel was pressing unobtrusively into his ribs. He glanced up, but Peter was still looking straight ahead at Geoffrey. "Oh, all right," he said. "I'm sorry. For goodness' sake come and put your old box back."

"Perhaps we could put the gun in there, too," Peter said. "With the eggs. That would keep the damp out all right. Would there be room?"

"I don't know. There might. Have to make sure it wouldn't break them." Geoffrey sat down again and fussed happily with his box and the hollows of crushed paper that held the small fragile birds' eggs, and Peter grinned over his head at Derek and bent down to hand over the gun.

The secret cupboard was not greatly secret, but not immediately visible either, being set in the angle between two walls of their almost-room, which by now they had christened the keep. They pushed their things as far back as they would go, and scattered grass and leaves over them as camouflage. Then they remembered Tom Hicks's advice and went into the back field with the spade head to find an offshoot of the brambles small enough to be transplanted to their camp entrance. They found one, eventually, but the job was more complicated than they expected, and it was only after much digging and groping and a great variety of scratches on arms and legs that they had a small bramble, with three sprawling arms, replanted in the Ditch. The long prickly arms, which they had hoped would wave menacingly in the air, lay drooping on the ground like lifeless snakes.

"D'you think it'll grow?"

"Looks dead already."

"P'r'aps we should water it."

There was a gloomy silence as they contemplated the journey across the field, over the fence, and down Derek's back garden, and the complications of explaining why they would want a bucket and some water.

"There's a tap on the allotments. But it's all the way over on the other side."

"We'd have to get a bucket anyway."

"Perhaps it'll rain."

"Listen!" Peter put up his hand, and they stopped obediently and listened, but there was nothing except the faint rumble of a truck on the distant main highway.

"What's up?"

"I thought I heard the pipe. From the anti-aircraft camp. Yes, listen, there it is again."

They could hear it now, coming in waves as the breeze caught it up and dropped some of it down: the hollow regular clatter as someone in that invisible camp, the real camp, which somehow they never even thought of as having the same name as their own, beat out the private signal of an impending air raid.

"It's the warning," Geoffrey said.

"No it isn't." Derek flapped one hand at him confidently. "It's their teatime. You always hear it in the afternoons. It just means someone's calling the soldiers to come and have a cuppa."

But then out of the gray day the other sound came whining, too, over the railway and the fields, past the floating silver barrage balloons, from the fire station in the village: the familiar, slow wailing whine, *eee—ow—eee—ow—eee—ow,* of the siren that was their own air-raid warning.

They made off like dutiful rabbits, over the fence, across the field and the garden, and each of them was breathless in his own house by the time the siren was slithering down its final dying wail out of the sky. And although the raid was more or less a false alarm for Everett Avenue, with only a very faint rumbling of bombs or guns a long way away and the all clear sending up its one long note very soon, they did not meet again that day, being kept at home by their mothers in case the warning should go again. But there was no other raid. A thin drizzle of rain came instead.

Derek spent the rest of the afternoon indoors building and rebuilding an airfield out of wooden blocks for Hugh tirelessly and joyfully to bomb with a toy plane; but he felt tranquil about it, with no sense of time running wasted away. After all, they had finished the camp. There it was, across the field, safe under its camouflage, waiting for them, looking after the six-shooter and the blowpipe and the birds' eggs. Or perhaps the gun and blowpipe and eggs were looking after the camp. It didn't matter. Either way it was there, and theirs. He felt old and fatherly playing with small Hugh, who could not understand such things.

6

Sunday

Sunday breakfast was scarcely over when Peter and Geoffrey came knocking at Derek's door.

"Let's go and get Tom," Peter said. "Show him the camp. He said he wanted to see it when it was finished."

"It rained last night. Shouldn't we go and check up first, to see if anything got washed away?"

"Ah no, it wasn't much. Look, the path's dry already. Come on."

They trooped out into Everett Avenue, absently kicking stones into puddles in the way that was forbidden as being hard on their shoes, and went up into the unfamiliar territory at the top of the road, past the Ditch on one hand and the White Road on the other. David Wiggs and a few of the White Road gang were kicking a ball about in the distance, halfway up the road, with a bigger boy lounging against a fence watching them, a boy so big that they would have taken him for Tom if that had not been unthinkable. David

Wiggs and his cronies yelled and capered and gibbered at them and were loftily ignored.

"Who's that boy?" Derek said.

"David Wiggs has a big brother," Peter said. "Must be him. Tommy hates him. I think they were at school together; they used to fight all the time. Tom said the Wiggs boy is older than him and he ought to be in the army, but he got out of it somehow, and he sells things on the black market instead."

"Bet that's what David Wiggs'll do, too."

They chanted the iniquities of the Wiggs family all the way to and through the Hickses' front gate, and then Geoffrey and Derek fell silent in the unfamiliarity of a strange house and garden. It was not a pretty garden. There were no crocuses or daffodils or shrubs as there were elsewhere in the road; only a small lawn bordered by blank flower beds. Tommy Hicks had no father, Derek remembered; he had died or vanished or something, years before.

Peter led them confidently to the back door and knocked. "Morning, Mrs. Hicks," he said to the turbaned head that appeared around the edge of the door. "Is Tommy there? It's me and Derry and Geoff, and we promised to show him something."

The head, which had looked anxious and cross, glanced briefly at all of them and then back to Peter, and softened into a faint smile. A hand appeared and smoothed back a few graying curls that had escaped from the turban. "All right, dear," said Mrs. Hicks. "I'll see."

They waited for what seemed a long time, and they

were sitting in a row on the back doorstep playing five-stones when Tom Hicks came out, combing his hair. "Gangway," he said, and he put the comb in his pocket and tipped Peter off the step with one foot. Peter rolled on the ground, with his arms wrapped around his head, and did an elaborate and noisy dying act. They saw Mrs. Hicks's head, anxious again, pop up at the window over the kitchen sink and disappear again.

"Hallo, Tom."

"We finished our camp. It's all done. Want to come and have a look?"

Derek added nervously, "If you've got time?"

"Sure," said Tom. "I've got time. Can't stay long, but I'll have a look-see. Shan't be long, Mum," he yelled into the kitchen, and the turban bobbed up and down.

They walked down Everett Avenue. David Wiggs and two other boys were sitting on the curb at the end of the White Road, whispering and sniggering; they glanced up and made derisive noises, and David Wiggs began chanting loudly, "Kitty cat, kitty cat, who's got the kitty cat—" The others joined in; and then they saw Tom, and their voices died away abruptly. They scrambled to their feet.

Tom stopped and looked at them. He said, "Hey, you."

David Wiggs's forelock fell lank and stringy down to his eyebrow. He wiped his nose on his wrist and tried to look belligerent. "What?"

"Sod off," Tom said.

He stood there casually with one hand in his pocket, towering over them all. The Wiggs boy and his friends paused resentfully for a moment, and then turned and ran; ran until they were halfway down their road in the safety of their own territory, where they turned to run backward, yelling inaudible insults as they went.

Geoffrey laughed. "That scared them."

"That Wiggs kid is just like his brother," Tom said, frowning after them, his face unreadable. Then he swung around. "Come on, then."

They made their way through Derek's garden, and as they reached the back door, John Brand came out in his slippers with some rubbish for the trashcan. "Well," he said. "Hallo, Tom. How are you? That's quite a procession you have there."

"Can we show Tom something in the back field, Dad?"

"Provided he throws you all over the fence," Mr. Brand said. "That might save it wobbling so much." He grinned at Tom. "I hear you're joining the Merchant Navy; is that right?"

"That's right. Quite soon now. My dad was a sailor. It runs in the family."

"I know he was," Mr. Brand said. "And a good one. Well, we shall all be thinking of you, Tom. And there are some of us old men who would give quite a bit to be with you."

"There's just as much to be done here," Tom said. "And it's just as dangerous."

He sounded somber and adult; the boys shuffled, fidgeting to get away. John Brand looked at them absently for a moment, as if they were not there. "Well, the very best of luck to you, Tom," he said, and they shook hands, and because of the uncomfortable gravity it was a release for Derek and Peter and Geoffrey to dance about Tom like sheepdog puppies, chivvying him down past the apple trees to the end of the garden. Derek said, as they crossed the back field, "We planted a bit of a blackberry bush at the entrance, like you said."

"It doesn't look too good, though. The rain might have helped it."

"We didn't half get scratched planting it. Look at that one." Peter pushed up one sleeve and waved an arm with a long dark scratch from elbow to wrist. "My mum made me change my shirt when I came in—there was blood all over the sleeve. She was wild."

"Well," Tom Hicks said gravely, "that shows your bramble's as good as barbed wire. It ought to keep any invaders out."

But he was wrong.

They saw nothing until they had crossed the stile onto the allotment field and then made the U-turn back, around the end of the tall wire-mesh fence and through the barbed wire, into the hummocks of the end of the Ditch. That was one of the good things about the camp, that you couldn't see it until you were almost on top of it. Derek was behind Peter and Geoff. Though he knew there was no need, he had paused solicitously to push down the top strand of barbed wire as Tom cocked his long leg over it. Grinning a little in anticipation, he watched them as he felt the straight part of the wire carve its rust-grained imprint into the palm of his hand. They bounded up onto the grassy hummock that ended the Ditch, from the top of which you looked down for the first time into the camp; and then for a long moment the world froze, and Derek pressed the wire harder into his hand—even though Tom was clear over it and standing at his side—as he saw Peter and Geoffrey stop up there as if they had run into a wall, stop stock-still gazing downward, and saw the change that came over their faces.

He was looking at Peter, and he never forgot what he saw on Peter's face. The cheerful eagerness died as if a light had been switched off, and for a second there was no expression at all, an utter emptiness, until the mouth twisted into any number of emotions and all of them black. It was like small Hugh's face after the moment between his falling down somewhere and feeling the pain that said he had hurt himself, when he opened his mouth in a wide downward arc and brought out first a choking silence and then a wild, unhappy yell. But Peter did not yell. He turned back to them and said gruffly, "Look," and Geoffrey turned, too, and Derek saw the same stricken look on his face.

He moved up with Tom and looked.

Their camp was no longer there. It had been wrecked with such savage thoroughness that it was difficult even to make out the outlines of the walls they had labored to build up. The hillock on which they stood, and which they had carved painstakingly into a sheer straight wall, slanted down now into a rough, lumpy slope. The far wall of the camp, with its battlements, was completely gone: flattened into a muddy mess of clay. The side wall of the Ditch, which they had carefully hollowed into the secret cupboard and wall of the keep, was pitted and gashed with what looked like the blows of a spade. The cupboard was gone, too, and so was the roof, and instead the whole of the bottom of the Ditch, which had been the floor of the camp and was now a muddy, trampled bog, was scattered with torn-up fragments of newspaper and splintered pieces of wood.

None of them said a word. They stood and looked.

The three-armed bramble that they had planted at the camp entrance lay feebly in the muddy chaos, torn into three pieces. Between the crushed branches there were the crumpled remnants of a cardboard box, and here and there broken pieces of eggshell. Scattered over these were other relics that Derek did not even recognize at first. Only when he stepped silently down, the first of all of them, and picked up an odd-looking giant splinter, did he see that his blowpipe and all its lovingly carved darts had been broken into very small pieces and dropped like confetti on top of the rest.

There was no sign anywhere of Peter's gun.

The thing that Derek noticed last of all was a thing that seemed to have no meaning: a small black heap that he took to be a wet crumpled rag, lying neatly in the very center of all the mess. His eyes and mind flickered on to it, and he wondered emptily where it had come from, and then he looked away again to a small blue-flecked fragment, pathetically delicate against the trampled orange mud, that he knew was a piece of Geoffrey's blackbird's egg. He stared down at it, not daring to look at any of the others. Peter stepped down beside him, slithering a little, and put one foot out gingerly to prod the crumpled black rag; Derek watched him, still numb.

Peter said, "It's the cat."

"The what?" Derek gazed blankly, uncomprehend-

ing; and as the toe of Peter's shoe gently stirred the heap, he saw first the frayed end of a dirty piece of rope, and then something that could have been the tip of a very small black nose. "Oh no," he said. "Oh, Pete, it can't be."

Geoffrey slipped down beside them. "Yes it is," he said.

"Is it dead?"

"Course it is."

"P'r'aps it's just hurt," Derek said, without hope. "It could be just unconscious. Couldn't it?"

Peter squatted down and put one hand gently on the small black heap. "Feel," he said.

Derek swallowed, and bent down and touched it, and felt the stiff curve of a small knobby backbone and wet fur that was very cold. He drew his hand back quickly and said, without any thought of shame, "I feel sick."

"Poor little cat," Peter said, and put one finger under a small dead paw.

"Who did it?"

They had almost forgotten Tom, and they started at the depth of his voice; he was standing above them on the hillock, the only one of them who had not moved since the first sight of the ruined camp. He looked very tall there above them, and squinting up at the sky behind him, they could not see the expression on his face. From where Derek stood, he could see next to Tom's head the floating outline of the nearest barrage balloon that hung on guard in the sky; he saw the two shapes next to one another against the curious brightness of the gray unbroken clouds, and together they looked funny, but it did not occur to him to laugh.

"Those kids," Peter said.

"The kids from the White Road," said Geoffrey. "It must have been."

Derek looked up at Tom and the barrage balloon, and he said, describing the memory as it came into his head, "We were coming out of the Ditch the other day, and we saw David Wiggs and his gang with a cat, a little black cat. They were holding it up by a rope and strangling it and poking it with sticks, and we chucked stones at them and the cat got away. And they were wild."

Geoffrey said, "And we saw them this morning with you, just now, remember?"

Just now, Derek thought; it seemed a hundred years away. He said slowly, "They were saying something about the cat—before you scared them off—and they were laughing."

"They were shouting at us on the way up, too," Peter said. "David Wiggs's brother was there with them then."

"Ah," Tom said softly. He came down the muddy slope into the camp, or what had been the camp, digging in his heels to avoid sliding, and he looked down at the cat. He said, "Someone must have drowned it."

"Oh no," Derek said quickly; he felt his throat jump at him again, and swallowed hard. "Wasn't—couldn't it just have got all wet in the rain?"

"Not that wet," Tom said. Then he stiffened and turned his head quickly. "What's that?"

They heard faint voices and laughter, and scrambled

up in time to see several figures running and leaping away toward Everett Avenue out of the front section of the Ditch, on the other side of the high impenetrable fence that ran parallel to the backs of the Everett Avenue gardens and cut the Ditch into two halves. The figures ran to a taller figure waiting for them at the end of the White Road, and waved mockingly back behind them, and disappeared.

"That's Johnny Wiggs up there," Tom said. He thrust both hands hard into his pockets and scowled. "That settles it."

"It was them, then," Peter said.

Geoffrey said bleakly, "I suppose they wanted to see how we looked when we found it all." He bent down and picked up the tiny curved piece of the broken blackbird's egg, and the splintered handle of one of Derek's darts, and looked across at the blank churned earth where the secret cupboard had been. Then his head jerked up. "Pete. Your gun. Where's your gun?"

Peter shrugged. "It's not here, is it? One of them must have taken it."

Geoffrey got up. "Well, you never know. They might have chucked it away." He began roving around the edges of the Ditch, peering into the grass.

"Beasts!" Derek burst out. "The mean dirty beasts!" He looked up at Tom. "It was such a good camp, it really was. We had it all finished up. And now we haven't even got a chance to use it once. We had some of Geoff's birds' eggs in the secret cupboard, and a blowpipe and darts I made, and Pete's six-shooter gun with the carved handle, and we left them here, and they just—" His voice wavered and disappeared, and he pointed miserably down at the litter on the mud.

"Well, they aren't going to get away with it," Tom said. "And we'll rebuild your camp and make it even better than it was."

"There's no point," Peter said drearily. "They'd only come sneaking in and bash it down again." He looked out down the Ditch toward the White Road, empty now except for two briskly walking housewives with shopping bags. "But if that David Wiggs has got my gun, he's jolly well going to give it back."

"He will," Tom said. "And they won't come near your camp again either. We'll show them."

"I don't see what we can do," Derek said. "We can't even fight them, not all at once—there's too many of them. Three against seven just isn't any good."

"Four against seven," Tom said.

There was a silence, and they stared at him.

Peter said, "But you aren't—they didn't—I mean, it's us they were getting at. You don't have to get into a fight because of us."

"That wouldn't be fair," Derek said. He added hastily, "Fair on you, I mean."

"I don't care," Tom said. "Anyway, you don't think those kids did this all on their own, do you? Johnny Wiggs is mixed up in it somehow. It wasn't any kid who drowned that cat. Or at any rate, they wouldn't have had the nice little idea of putting it here for you to find. If you ask me, they need to be taught a lesson. All of them. I watched you making that camp of yours."

"Hey!" Geoffrey came jumping down from the far side of the Ditch, where he had been poking about beside the fence. "Look, I found this in the grass over there; they must have just buzzed it away. But there isn't any sign of your gun, Pete."

He was holding their old broken spade, which had been stowed in the secret cupboard with all the rest. They had left it clean, after rubbing it carefully with handfuls of grass. Now it was caked thickly with hunks of damp mud.

Geoffrey rubbed his finger down the spade, sending down a shower of muddy flakes. He said without looking up, "Um—I thought, if we've got this to dig with —perhaps we could bury the cat."

There was a short silence. Then Peter said briskly, "Good idea."

"Are you really sure it's dead?" Derek looked again at the small black heap.

Tom picked it up. The body, as it suddenly became, was stiff and very small in his large hand. "Quite sure," he said. "Come on, then. Dig a hole. Over here."

They buried the cat close to the tall fence and the bramble thicket, in a spot where no one normally would walk; they had first to dig out several hummocks of grass and a great many tough, stringy roots, and when they had finished, they replaced the grass so that even they had difficulty in seeing the place. Derek wondered whether they should not have had some sort of ceremonial, but hadn't the nerve to say so. It was Peter who provided a kind of substitute: he stamped down the grass with his heel, stepped back, and said bitterly, "At least now maybe they'll leave the poor thing in peace."

"We ought to challenge them to a battle," Geoffrey said.

"I'll tell you what we'll do," said Tom. He smoothed a patch of earth with his foot, took a piece of Derek's broken blowpipe, and drew some lines. "You wouldn't know this," he said, "because you live in the wrong bit of the road. But this line here, see, is the end of the back gardens of the houses on the White Road. And here at this end of it, the line going off at a right angle, is the end of my back garden. Our back fence overlooks their back fences, and from my bedroom window I can see whatever's going on in their back gardens. And all this space on the other side of the fences, between the houses and the railway line, is the field where the anti-aircraft camp is."

They stirred with interest. "I never knew that," Peter said.

"Well, you can't see much because the field's full of trees and bushes, and anyway the camp's a fair way off in the middle of it and all wired off. Nobody can get near it. Actually nobody's supposed to even go in the field at all—there are notices all over—but those White Road kids go there all the time."

"I never really thought where they went apart from the road," Derek said. "I thought it was just their own gardens." Now that he came to think about it, he realized he had never wondered very much about the Children from the White Road at all.

"Well, listen anyway," Tom said. "The point is this. The Wiggs garden is about halfway up the White Road, and their back fence has been all broken down for ages. It leans right down to the ground in the middle, and they can just walk out into the field over it. Old man Wiggs is away half the time driving his truck, and anyway he's a lazy old bugger and he's never done anything to mend the fence. So the Wiggs boys have propped up one bit of it and turned it into a kind of hut, and they use that as their base. All the White Road kids do. It's their camp, if you like. Just the same as yours. Or the same as yours would have been. They keep all kinds of stuff in there; I've watched them from the top window sometimes. And they have an old tarpaulin over the bit of the fence that makes their roof. I don't know where that came from; I dare say they pinched it from someone."

Geoffrey said enviously, "It sounds a jolly good way of making a camp."

Peter looked down at Tom's drawing and rubbed the scar on his nose. "You mean, if they've wrecked our camp, then we could wreck theirs?"

Derek made an uneasy sound of protest and felt ashamed of it, but still uneasy.

Tom glanced at him. "Well," he said noncommittally, "it's worth thinking about."

"We couldn't just sneak in when they weren't there and knock it down," Derek said. "I mean, that wouldn't be fair."

"I don't see why not," said Geoffrey. "That's just what they did to us."

"I know they did." Derek fidgeted, trying to find words. "But that's why. I mean, they're sneaky and we aren't. I mean, we don't pinch other people's things, like Pete's six-shooter, and drown cats just for fun. So we have to do something different."

Peter said reasonably, "Well, we can't attack their

camp when they're in it. That would be just as hopeless as trying to fight them anywhere else."

"Yes," Tom said. "But there are all sorts of ways of attacking. You don't always have to just run up and jump on someone. They're always going out from their camp into the big field. We could ambush them on their way back."

"Ambush?"

"I told you there were lots of trees. Lots of cover. They'd never see us until it was too late."

"Mud-balls," said Geoffrey.

"What?" said Tom.

"Mud-balls." Geoffrey looked at the other two, and they looked at him, and each of them stooped to the trampled wall of their lost camp and picked up a double handful of red-brown sticky mud and shaped it into a ball.

"Watch," Peter said. He swung back his arm, and the mud-ball went sailing heavily through the air to the back fence of the house on the other side of the Ditch, where it exploded in a dull squelch to leave a flattened muddy patch on the dark wood. Derek and Geoffrey sent theirs flying after it, and there were three orange patches messily scarring the wood.

"We had a mud-ball fight once, in the other bit of the Ditch," Derek said in happy remembering. "It was smashing. But we all got into such a row that we've never been able to do it again. You end up in an awful mess."

"I can imagine," Tom said. He dug his fingers into the mud of the Ditch and looked at it thoughtfully.

"Clay. Sticky. Funny, there isn't any of it anywhere else around here. The soil in our garden is more like gravel. It is in the big field, too, and up there." He gestured widely at the rows of seedlings in the cabbage field and the dark turned earth.

"So it is in our garden," said Derek. "And on the allotments. My dad says the Ditch is clay because they went so deep when it was first dug. He says there's a layer of clay down underneath everything around here, but that you never see it usually because it's all covered up with other sorts of earth. And I asked Mrs. Wilson once in geography, and she said so, too."

"Mud-balls," Tom said. He grinned at them. "How do you think the Wiggs kids would look covered in mud?"

"They wouldn't half get into trouble," Geoffrey said.

Peter said, with rising enthusiasm, "We could make lots of mud-balls here, hundreds of them, and take them up to your field."

"And have stacks of them behind a tree," Derek said.

"And ambush them."

"When they'd be coming back to their camp to go home for tea or something—all of a sudden—splat!"

"And their camp, too. Everything all covered with mud."

Geoffrey said hopefully, "Tomorrow? It's Easter holiday this week."

"Tomorrow morning," Tom said.

7

Monday

They began their preparations the next morning and went on for most of the day. After some discussion of their own past mud fight, they had decided that it would be better not to make the mud-balls in advance, but to transport a stock of clay ready to be molded into ammunition on the spot. If you made mud-balls too soon, they reminded one another, they would either ooze into flat nothings or dry out enough to break into useless bits. The business of carrying clay from the Ditch to the battlefield was a problem, but only until Tom miraculously produced a wheelbarrow from his garden shed. They wondered what his mother would say, but they had seen her going down the road early in the morning, carrying a shopping bag, and they did not ask. In any case, one did not ask Tommy Hicks about things; he was the man of his house.

It was a gray day again, and for most of the morning few people were visible in the road. They filled the wheelbarrow laboriously with mud three times, digging it from their old original campsite in the front half of the Ditch and wheeling it up Everett Avenue to the front gate of Tom's house. They peered carefully each time down into the White Road as they passed, but there was no sign at all of the Wiggs boys and their gang.

"They're back there in their camp," Peter said.

Geoffrey said, giggling nervously, "They wouldn't be if they knew."

The arrival of the wheelbarrow was the most nerve-twitching moment each time. Tom would be waiting for them in his front garden, take it from them, and disappear. He said he had a way from his garden to what he called the point of ambush. They had no idea what he meant, but they waited quietly in his garden until he came back again with the empty barrow and the spade, which he had provided, at the same time.

Peter said once, "Don't you think people must be wondering what we're doing?"

"If anybody asks," said Tom, "I'm just taking a bit of earth from the Ditch to put in the garden, and you're helping me."

"There's nobody about anyway," Derek said easily, though he knew he was the most nervous of them all.

"Isn't there any way we could bring it without anyone seeing?"

Tom said, "The only other way is the way the White Road kids must have gone when they went to raid your camp."

They stared at him. After a moment Peter said, "Isn't that nutty? We never even wondered. How could they have got there? They couldn't just have come up straight through the Ditch from Everett, because the big fence cuts across it between the ends of the back gardens."

"That was why we thought it was a good place for a camp in the beginning," Derek said gloomily.

"I worked it out," Tom said. "I reckon they just came up to the end of Everett, outside my house, and over the gate into the big field and around the backs of the Everett Avenue houses through the cabbages. Easy. All they had to do was make sure none of the soldiers happened to be watching them."

They took two more loads across the road, and when the last was delivered, Tom took them with him to see the point of ambush. He showed them a break in his own back garden fence, and beyond it, in the big tree-scattered field that they had never seen before, a thicket of scrub and bushes in the middle of which they could just make out a reddish-brown glimmer that was the heap of mud from the Ditch. It was clear that the heap could only be visible from where they stood; the thicket seemed to curve toward them in a sort of arc, and the thick tangle of branches and trunks would easily shield anything within the arc from being seen by even the keenest eyes looking from the other side.

Derek saw this and approved it, but at the same time he reflected with a faint sinking feeling that this ideal thicket seemed to be a very long way from Tom's garden fence. To reach it, they would have to cross a lot of open field. He looked across to the left at the back fences of the houses of the White Road, lined there with the untidy, unbeautiful, somehow private look that the backs of houses always have. When he found the fence that was bent downward, a break in the long line, and must therefore belong to the Wiggs house, he thought that it seemed very likely indeed that the Wiggs gang could, if they were looking, have an easy view of anyone crossing the field from Tom's house to the curving thicket.

He said, "Are you sure you really got it all over there without them seeing you? I mean with the wheelbarrow and all, weren't you awfully easy for them to spot from over there?"

Tommy Hicks grinned. "You'd be surprised," he said. "I used to get across this field every day without being seen when I was a kid your age, and there's a lot more cover now than there was then. Now listen. The first bit is the most difficult, after you've got out through the fence into the field. Nobody can see you while you're actually getting out, because the top corner of our garden blocks the view, but after that you have to dart very quickly for a yard or two to get to the first bit of cover. That is, you have to dart, run for it, if you're my size, but four people running across one after the other would be a bit of a risk, and I reckon you three are small enough to do it better by wriggling through the grass. Indian style. Are you good at that?"

"Course," they said, not without pride.

He looked from one to another of them and nodded seriously, though Derek had the feeling he would have preferred to be laughing at them. Or perhaps not; he was obviously enjoying all of this quite as much as they were.

"Well," Tom said. "I'll go first. This is a practice

run. Derek, you come after me. Then Geoff, then Pete. We go from one bit of cover to the next, and each of you must watch the one in front of him very carefully to see where he goes to and how he does it. And copy it exactly. Specially you, Derek, because you'll be watching me and sending back what I do, and I'm the only one who knows the way. You watch me get to the first cover, and then the second, and when I'm there, you leave here for the first. Then when I see you're at the first, I leave the second for the third, and when I'm there, you leave for the second. And so on. The same for all of you. All right? That means that each of us is always one stage away from the one in front. It sounds a bit slow, but there isn't enough room behind each bit of cover for more than one person, so the first one has to leave it before the next one gets there."

"Um," Geoffrey said doubtfully.

"Oh, come on," Pete said. "That's not hard."

"Sounds awful complicated."

"Only the first time," Tom said. "Try it anyway. All right? Here we go then."

He squeezed out through the gap in the planks and crouched at the other side of the fence; the others stood back so that Derek had a clear view of him. The way was a surprise from the beginning; Tom slipped suddenly sideways, to the right, as if he were making not for the thicket but almost in the opposite direction. Derek saw him run, crouching low, and pause beside a bush that was not much bigger than he was himself—"That's the first piece of cover," he thought—and then drop to his hands and knees and crawl rapidly through the long grass to a group of three small trees. Once he was there, they could no longer see him, but it was obviously the second stage.

"Go on, Derry," Peter said.

Derek slipped through the gap in the fence, smelling the faint, friendly creosote smell of the thin planks. He stood nervous and excited in the field, and heard the blood thump in his neck, and glanced over at the mysterious wired-in shape of the anti-aircraft camp at the far side of the field: even if the Wiggs gang couldn't see them, would one of the soldiers notice them and come running from there? Pushing the idea away, he fixed his eyes on the bush that was his first landmark, dropped to the ground, and wriggled through the damp grass with the side-to-side snake crawl that was, they had long ago discovered from experience rather than lessons, the only way to stalk without having your bottom sticking conspicuously up in the air. He was so intent on perfecting his wriggle that he ran his face into the bush before he realized that he was there, and jerked sideways. Prickles: of course, it was a hawthorn bush. Probably most of the bushes and trees in this field would be hawthorn; that, with the brambles, was the only thing that grew in his own back field. Raising his head, he saw Tom, clearly visible now, move on from the group of trees in another zigzagging direction that would bring him closer to the thicket; almost as soon as he started, he was cut off from view by the trees, and Derek felt a moment's panic and began wriggling hastily off again in his wake. Now that he was away from the shelter of the fence, the field seemed very open; he felt that anything could at any moment pounce on him from above. But at the same moment he realized that there was no danger after all of losing the way, even with Tom out of sight; the passing to and fro of the wheelbarrow had flattened the grass and weeds along this way

to the thicket so that it was as clearly marked as a rabbit's path. Here and there he could even see a few clumps of mud that must have dribbled off the load in the barrow. Reaching the trees, he glanced up and saw Tom peering back at him from behind a gigantic clump of nettles. Looking back at the fence, a long way away now, he saw Peter standing waiting to leave the gap. Geoff was presumably somewhere in the middle. It was like a chain. Tom vanished again, and Derek crawled on more confidently.

When he reached the thicket, he found the cover was so dense that Tom was standing casually upright beside the damp mound of clay. Derek got up, rubbing his grass-green hands and knees, and grinned in triumph. Geoffrey wriggled up, and then Peter, and they squatted in a row looking about them in pleased discovery. It was like being in a ship at sea. They were almost in the middle of the field, with acres of open space on every side of them; the thicket was the size of a small house and made up of hawthorn trees and scrub so closely tangled that it was obviously impossible for anyone to spot them from any direction except the one from which they had come.

Tom said, "That was good. I couldn't even see you when I looked back. Nothing moving at all. You'd all make good commandos."

They tried to look modest. Peter said, "This is a smashing place for an ambush. Or it's like a fort, a castle; you could be besieged in it, and nobody could get at you except from the back."

"I don't see how we ambush them, though." Geoff peered ahead through the branches. "I can see the place where their camp is, but we can't throw mud-balls that far. I mean, all they have to do is retreat to it, and we can't get at them without going out into the open."

"Well, I daresay they will retreat in the end," said Tom. "But with any luck we'll have got them lovely and muddy before then. See, I've watched those kids for years from our house. I know what they usually do. They don't just hang around inside their camp all the time any more than you would; they play in this field the way you do in yours. And once they're out, they're an easy shot from here, and if they're caught out past these trees, they have to pass pretty close to them before they can get back to their garden. There isn't any other way. You look."

Through the gaps in the trees, narrow indeed as castle windows, they saw that he was right. Between the backs of the White Road houses on one side and the remnants of an ancient orchard that joined the field to the railway line on the other, there was only an open strip of land with scarcely any protection except a few odd patches of brambles. From their thicket they could land a shot on anyone within that open strip. And if the White Road gang were out, the interesting trees of the old orchard made the most obvious place for them to go—and to get to and from those trees, they should have to cross the open land.

"Suppose they decide to come and spend the day in here?" Geoffrey said.

Tom nodded casually. "They do sometimes. That's why it's all trodden down inside. We just have to make sure that we're in here first. Then if they do come in this direction, that's all the better; we'll have them on a plate."

"We'll be here first all right," Derek said.

8

Tuesday

They were there first. They were there very shortly after breakfast, knocking self-consciously at the back door of Tom's house, each arguing with the others in violent whispers over the best way to apologize to Mrs. Hicks if they had waked her up. But there was no need. When Tom came to the door, pushing his fingers sleepily through his short curly hair as if it were a hearthrug, he said that his mother was working an early shift at one of the factories and that she had already been gone for an hour.

"Come on in for a minute," he said.

They stood in an awkward group in the small kitchen, waiting while he rinsed a plate and a cup at the sink. There was a coal stove in one corner, of the kind that all their own houses had, serving both to warm the kitchen and to heat the water supply. Tom bent down and shut its draft door when he had finished at the sink; his most casual actions seemed odd to them, like those not of a boy but of a grown man, the kind of things that their fathers would naturally do. Derek looked curiously around the kitchen and saw on one wall a picture frame that held not a picture but a printed notice. It said: *We are not interested in the possibilities of defeat. They do not exist.*

"That means the war, of course," Tom said, watching him.

The others looked. "Did Churchill say that?" said Peter.

"I don't think so," Tom said. "I think it was someone a long time ago. Mr. Churchill says some pretty good things, though. Like the Dunkirk speech."

He looked at them expectantly.

"Um," said Derek.

Geoffrey nodded, but prudently said nothing. Peter, more courageous, said, "What Dunkirk speech?"

Tom frowned. "You ought to know it by heart," he said, and he seemed even more like somebody's father. He went back to the sink and washed his hands, and stood there with one hand on the faucet, looking out of the window. He said: *"We shall go on to the end, we shall fight in France, we shall fight on the seas and oceans, we shall fight with growing confidence and growing strength in the air, we shall defend our island, whatever the cost may be, we shall fight on the beaches, we shall fight on the landing grounds, we shall fight in the fields and in the streets, we shall fight in the hills."* He paused. *"We shall* never *surrender,"* he said.

There was a short silence.

"I do remember it now," Derek said slowly. "I remember my father reading it to us."

"I heard Mr. Churchill saying it, on the radio,"

Geoffrey said at once. Then he saw Tom's eyebrows go up and added hastily, "At least I think I did."

"You couldn't have heard Churchill," said Tom. "He said that in the House of Commons."

Derek was trying to think backward; he could remember John Brand standing proud and serious in the living room reading to them from the newspaper, but it seemed a long time ago. He said, "Wasn't there more of it than that?"

"Lots more before it. But only one other bit at the end."

Clearly Tom had the bit at the end in his head, too. It was Peter again who said, "What was that?"

"We shall never surrender," Tom said again, *"and even if, which I do not for a moment believe, this island or a large part of it were subjugated and starving, then our empire beyond the seas, armed and guarded by the British Fleet, would carry on the struggle, until, in God's good time, the New World, with all its power and might, steps forth to the rescue and the liberation of the Old."*

"The New World?" said Derek. He had forgotten that.

"America," Tom said.

"Oh yes, of course."

"We had a food parcel from America last month," Peter said. "Through someone at my dad's firm. There was a super cake in it."

Derek said with enthusiasm, "And your mum gave mine the sausages, remember? We had them for supper. They were the best sausages I've ever tasted. They must have some smashing kinds of food in America."

Tom said suddenly, "An awful lot of our ships are being sunk carrying food like that from America. And fuel, and steel and things. When I'm on one, I'll probably be sunk before long, too. They say you're lucky if you last out more than two convoys."

Sobered, they stared at him; he was still gazing fiercely out of the window at nothing. For a moment he was like someone from another planet, someone they had never seen before. He said, as if to himself, "Somebody has to sail the ships. *We shall fight on the seas and oceans,* Mr. Churchill said. *We shall never surrender.* Somebody has to go and get the things to do the fighting with. And people like that Johnny Wiggs, they don't care about that, so long as they can sit on their fat behinds at home and dodge everything. You don't catch people like Johnny Wiggs joining up or getting drafted, oh no. He isn't even in the Home Guard; d'you know that? But he's old enough. He's six months older than I am."

He stopped, abruptly, and swung around and grinned at them. "Come on, then," he said. "You have to be out early for an ambush. And just keep your fingers crossed that it doesn't rain."

They trooped outside silently; Tom locked the back door behind them and put the key under a flowerpot beside the door. "Not that a burglar would get much joy out of our house," he said.

The sky was a solid gray sheet of cloud. "It does look like rain," Geoff said. "And it rained a little bit again in the night—you can tell."

"That's why there wasn't a raid," Tom said.

"It'll have made our clay pile just gooey enough for making good mud-balls," Peter said with relish.

"Sssh," Derek said. They had arrived at the gap in the fence.

Tom said, "Here we go. Same rules. But you know the way this time."

Knowing the way, Derek found, was both a good thing and a bad. He was the last in line this time, and as he wriggled from one piece of cover to the next, he felt even more exposed, knowing that if anyone were following them, he, Derek, would be the first one to be grabbed. He knew that there was no one following, of course—he looked behind him frequently, to check—but that made no difference to the empty feeling in his throat. The journey was not for practice this time; this was the real thing. The top of Geoff's dark head bobbed now and again through the grass and scrub ahead of him, and he kept moving to stay as close as he dared. Just before the last stage of the zigzag path, he put the heel of his hand down hard on a thorn, said aloud without thinking, *"Ow,"* and dropped flat in panic at the sound of his own voice. But it had seemed loud only to him; when he crawled up—slowly and casually this time—to join the others in the hollow thicket, they showed no sign of having heard.

They waited there, squatting on the bare ground. There was not much grass inside the thicket, but only a black, granular earth crisscrossed with the thin roots of the hawthorns. They took turns at standing cramped inside the prickly depths of the largest bush, to keep watch on the back of the Wiggs boys' house. Those not on watch kept an eye on the rest of the field all around, but there was no movement anywhere, even in the distant hump of the anti-aircraft camp. The morning crept past, and the cloud-roof of the sky began to break up so that patches of blue showed here and there, and a glimpse sometimes of a watery sun. In the first half of the morning they worked out in hopeful detail their plan of attack. They would wait until the Wiggs gang were out in the middle of the field and on their way, it was to be hoped, to the old orchard or the railway line or anything on the opposite side of the field from their house. Then at a signal from Tom, they would unleash their ambush. Tom would break a quick gap through the thinnest part of the thicket, where only slender arms of hawthorn spread up and out, giving cover enough now but easily enough trampled down when the time came; and through this gap they would send a fusillade of mud-balls, with any luck catching the enemy so much unawares that they would be coated with mud before they realized what was happening.

"We ought to make a whole lot of mud-balls in advance," Geoff said.

"They'd dry out," said Peter. "And they just fall to bits when they do that."

"We could put grass in them—like bricks. They put straw in bricks to make them hold together, my dad says."

Tom, listening to their muttering from where he stood on watch, glanced back over his shoulder. "You do that, and your mud-balls'd dry out just like bricks, too. Then someone would get hurt, and there'd be trouble."

They sat thinking. Derek leaned out beyond the edge of the trees for a piece of grass to chew, pulling the stem slow and steady so that it slid tender-tipped out of its sheath without bringing the root with it. "We could make a lot very quickly at the last minute," he said, "as soon as we spotted them. Then there wouldn't be time for the mud to dry, but they'd be ready. We could even have one person doing nothing but make ammunition to hand to the others to throw. Take turns."

"That's a good idea," said Tom. He turned back and peered again through the branches and then stiffened. He said softly, without turning around, "You'd better start making them now.

They scrambled cautiously to their feet and looked for gaps in the thicket to try and catch a glimpse of the Wiggs fence. With twigs pricking against his face, Derek saw the figures moving around the broken section of the fence that was the camp's roof; one boy was crawling inside, handing out something to another; three or four others were scuffling in the grass, and a taller boy that could only be Johnny Wiggs, the elder brother, was leaning against the fence watching them.

"Come on," Peter hissed urgently, and then bent and began shaping handfuls of the clay from the great orange heap into rough finger-marked balls and laying them in rows along the near edge of the heap. Once they had begun the familiar process, they fell easily into a quick, practiced series of movements; scoop up a handful of mud, cup it in your hand, cup the other hand over the top and squeeze, so that a little brown water trickled through the fingers, give the ball a half-turn, and squeeze again to make sure it would keep its shape, at least for as long as would be necessary. And then put it down and begin again.

"Are they really going to come out, Tommy?" Geoff said.

"Can't tell. I think they are." Tom moved across to the thin edge of the thicket and began gently, quietly, breaking down layers of the slender branches so that there would be only a last fragile border of cover to break through when the moment came to launch their attack. Derek heard the blood thumping in his ears with anticipation and nervousness, and tried to bury his excitement in the work of making ammunition.

"You seem to make them quickest, Derry." Tom was looking back at them briefly again. "You keep on for a bit when the rest of us start to throw. Then you take over, Geoff, and then Pete. Or two of you at once if we seem to be running out. You'll have to keep an eye on how much we use." He looked back and waved an arm at them behind his back. "Stop for a minute, stay quiet. They're coming."

The sun was shining properly now, dappling the dark hollow of the thicket with patterns of light through the leaves; the field was very quiet, but they could hear the voices of the Wiggs gang calling indistinctly to one another. They crouched there, mute. The voices grew louder, nearer. They heard one shout, louder than the rest, "Aw come *on,* Johnny, just for a bit." Derek was squatting behind the mud pile, one knee sunk in the wet clay where he had been leaning over to drop mud-balls scooped from the top into the pile on the other side. He could see nothing outside from there, but in front of him he saw Pete bob suddenly in excited delight and knew that the enemy must all be within range, exposed out there in the middle of the empty field.

Without turning, Tom shot out one arm and grabbed Geoffrey and put him in position at his side; then waved at Peter to make a third in line. Derek woke suddenly out of paralysis and began frenziedly making more mud-balls and dropping them down onto the pile, rather resenting his dull job behind the lines. After all, he could throw farther and harder than Geoff. But there was no time for thinking. Tom suddenly let out a great whoop and crashed trampling through the last few saplings, with Geoff and Pete at his side prancing and yelling, each with an armful of mud-balls clutched between crooked forearm and dirty shirt, and the battle was on.

Derek paused long enough to see the thicket break in half as the three figures trod and jumped a great gap through the middle; long enough to see arms jerk back and throw, and at least two White Road boys out in the middle of the field stumble and spin as a splattering handful of mud hit them on chest or back. Then he worked away at the making, and before his face the hands of Tom and Pete and Geoffrey came down and back and down and back snatching up more ammunition for the battle. He thought: "Someone's throwing straight, anyway. Tom, and Pete; and maybe even Geoff's doing all right." He could hear voices yelling in confusion, curses and angry roars from the field, and shrieks of delight from above his head. And then suddenly it was too much for him; he wanted to be part

of it. There was still a good-sized heap of mud-balls waiting after all; and he snatched up an armful and yelled, "Someone else's turn," and jumped forward to stand between Tom and Pete and send his own ammunition flying out at the running figures in the field.

Nobody else did take a turn; there was no time and no need. The boys from the White Road were scattering away from the thicket; two of them back to their camp, the rest in the opposite direction, to the far side of the field. Derek hurled his mud-balls; nothing could have stopped him from throwing all he had. Only one of them found a mark, and that only on the ankle of one flying form. Still, the sight even of that small brown splash of mud was a satisfaction.

They stopped throwing. All the targets were out of range. Across the field beside the crooked old trees of the disused orchard, the escaped enemy drew together in a little group around the taller figure of Johnny Wiggs. The two boys cut off on the other side were no longer visible, but presumably sheltering inside their camp.

"Those two," Tom said, squatting down but keeping a wary eye on the far group. "We'll have to watch out for them. They might try going back through their garden to the road and coming into the field behind us."

"They couldn't," Geoff said. "They wouldn't go through your house, and the gate to the field's all padlocked and wired, because of the anti-aircraft camp."

"They might all the same."

"What are the rest doing over there?" Peter peered across at the main group.

Tom grinned. "Trying to wipe off some of the mud, I expect."

"What happens next?" said Derek.

There was a pause, and they looked out at the knot of distant figures and then back at Tom. In all their enthusiastic discussion of plans for the ambush, it had not occurred to them that the battle would have a second stage. Their imagining had begun and ended with the throwing of their mud-balls and the discomfiture of the unsuspecting enemy. They had never thought beyond that. The ambush was to be their great action, the wreaking of vengeance for the shattered camp and the killed cat. Now that it was over, what were they to do next?

Geoffrey was still watching the group across the field. "They've split up," he said. "Two of them have gone off into the trees."

Peter said, carefully casual, "I suppose they're planning a counterattack."

Derek swallowed and said the thing that he knew they were all thinking but that it seemed shameful to say aloud. "Tom? Do we call it quits and go back to your garden now, or do we stay here and wait to see what they do?"

The others looked at him, and he looked at them, and while his last words were still in his ears, he said the other thing he knew they were feeling as well.

"Seems awfully soft, really, just to go back. Almost like running away."

That was it, they knew. If the White Road gang had run from the ambush back to their own camp and disappeared into its safe shelter, that would have been one thing. Left victorious, they could have retired: holders of the field, avengers of the original sneak attack. But the White Road gang hadn't disappeared; they were still out there in the field, muddy and glaring, and obviously planning an attack of a different kind. If the ambushers were to leave the stage now, they would not be retiring in victory; they would be beating a retreat.

That wouldn't do at all.

Tom said softly, contentedly, almost crooning, "They'll be back. We've only just begun."

Peter and Derek and Geoffrey looked at him, but not at one another. They were trying to grasp the shift in roles. Before, they had been in the position of advantage: the ambushers, with surprise and shelter on their side. Now they were about to become the besieged. They would still have the shelter of the thicket, but unless they were watchful and lucky, the advantage of surprise would belong now to the other side. It was beginning to seem unlikely that they would come out of this next encounter unscathed.

Derek thought: "It's really just the same as if we'd challenged them in the first place."

Peter took a deep breath. "If they're going to come after us, we'd better have a lot more ammunition ready."

"Too true," Tom said.

He stood keeping watch on the field, and they worked away steadily at the dwindling heap of clay. Neat rows and mounds of mud-balls rose all around it until they were higher than the clay that remained.

Tom glanced back. "That'll do," he said. "Keep

watch instead. They've all split up now and gone under cover. You come over here, Pete, level with me, and you two over there with your backs to us. Then we'll be watching the whole field. If you spot anyone, yell, and open fire if they're in range. And whoever's nearest can help. But the other two will have to stay keeping watch, because they're bound to attack from at least two places at once."

They squatted there in the thicket, four corners of an outward-facing square, and waited. The field seemed quite empty and very peaceful. Though they could feel only a gentle breeze stirring the branches of the hawthorns now and again, the clouds above were scudding along at a great pace: ragged, misty-edged gray clouds from the mass that had brought the rain of the night before. In the silence below the sky, Derek listened so hard that he felt his ears should be pricked high and alert like a dog's; but he could hear nothing except the quarreling of starlings in some distant tree.

He stared out at the field, moving his eyes to and fro across his allotted segment of horizon and back again, but he still could see nothing except the new grass and the scattered bushes and trees and, away beyond them, the barbed-wire fence of the anti-aircraft camp.

Without moving his gaze he said softly to Geoff, close beside him and watching another quarter of the compass, "What d'you think they'll do?"

"Dunno. Rush us, I suppose. Try to jump on us quick and give us a bashing." There was a moment's pause, and he added, without much hope, "Or they might just have gone away and gone home."

Derek said gloomily, "Fat chance."

They waited and watched. Behind them in the thicket Derek could hear a rustle of voices as Tom and Peter talked, but he could not distinguish the words.

Beside him Geoffrey said quietly, so quietly that he could barely hear him either, "Derry? I don't like this much."

The naked honesty of it was something not often heard from someone like Geoff, and for that moment Derek liked him more than he had ever liked him before. He said truthfully, "Neither do I."

Suddenly there was a shout behind them, splitting the day into splinters, a cry of "There they go! Look there!" and a scuffle of rapid movement. Derek swung around and saw Tom halfway to his feet and Peter dancing uncontrollably up and down and hurling mudballs toward the camp in the Wiggs boys' back fence. Beyond, and quite close to the thicket, two figures were weaving and ducking and trying unsuccessfully to run on through the defensive barrage of splattering handfuls of mud. He swung his gaze guiltily back to his own ward as Tom joined in the throwing, and he realized how vulnerable every other direction had become.

It was almost too late. In the instant that he turned back, he heard Geoff hiss, "What's that?"

Wildly he stared out at the field and caught sight first of one flicker of movement and then another, and then a third; all in line and all horribly near, not more than twenty yards away. The Wiggs boys and their gang must have been stalking them, slowly and carefully, all this while, spread out in line across this part of the field so that no more than one head at any point was using the scanty clumps of scrub for cover. He knew that it would be disastrous to let them get even one step closer.

"Quick!" he said hoarsely, and swung around, waving at Geoff to do the same, and grabbed up an armful of mud-balls so large that he could scarcely hold them. And then he was up on his feet, whooping and yelling as Peter had done, and hurling ammunition—not too fast, not too fast, don't waste it—out at the places where they had seen the heads move.

In an instant Geoffrey was throwing, too, and their speed worked. At the sound of the shouting, the besiegers assumed they had all been seen, and they scrambled up out of their cover and ran headlong into the barrage.

"Tom!" Derek shrieked, and went on throwing. There were five of them coming, running, ducking and dodging, and the middle figure of the five and the first to have risen to his feet was big Johnny Wiggs, hurtling toward them and looking twice as big as Tom and as menacing as a runaway tank. Instinctively Derek used him as a target, and one mud-ball—he never knew whether it was his own or Geoff's—caught Johnny Wiggs on the side of the chin and sent him staggering comically backward with splashes of mud all over his face and shirt. The other boys, smaller, two of them smaller even than Derek and Geoff, paused as they glimpsed his stumbling and looked first at him and then ahead at the thicket. The pause was enough for Derek and Geoffrey, and now Peter joining them as well, to take better aim and send them, too, ducking to the ground. So the first charge had been stopped, even though the chargers were nearer now than they had been before.

But not for long; for not more than the few seconds in which Peter and Derek and Geoffrey took breath and grinned at one another in excitement and triumph. Johnny Wiggs scrambled to his feet, and with him his followers, and though the barrage from the thicket began hastily again, there is only so much that a few thrown mud-balls can do to stop five charging boys, especially when only three boys are doing the throwing. Tom was still busy behind them in the thicket, trying to keep off the first two attackers, who were coming again now, with wary arms crooked over their charging heads so that even the most accurate mud-ball could do very little to stop them at all.

Still, as Derek happily noticed in the moment before battle broke loose, they were all very muddy indeed.

Then the charge hit the thicket, and the besiegers were on top of the ambushers, and Derek was rolling on the ground twisting wildly to keep off the flailing form of David Wiggs, barely recognizable through the great orange smear of clay across one side of his face. Dimly through the confusion he was aware that two largish boys were trying to pin Pete to the ground, and two smaller ones were thumping at a wriggling Geoff, and that big Johnny Wiggs was standing in the midst of it all glaring down at them with both his fists clenched. Then David Wiggs's elbow poked Derek in the eye, and the pain of it was so sudden and infuriating that he gave a great jerk upward and in a wrathful instant found himself sitting on David Wiggs's chest, bringing his knees forward to pin the flapping elbows down.

David Wiggs said furiously and indistinctly, "Get off!" and brought his legs up to kick at Derek's back; but it was another pair of hands that pulled Derek off, as one of the boys attacking Pete left off to come to the rescue. And then the whole thrashing grunting confusion began again, and all of it far nastier than any fight Derek and Peter and Geoff had ever had among themselves, because each of the members of this battle was very angry and wrought-up, and each of them had a grievance that he was remembering with every twist and punch. It was not a very clear remembering, but the grievance was nonetheless there. If Derek had ever been excited enough to enjoy it at the beginning, he was not enjoying it a very few seconds after it had begun, and even less when it had been going on its scrambling, battering way for longer than that.

Somebody sat down hard on his legs, to join the somebody else who seemed to be sitting on his shoulders, and he grunted into the grass. All around it was now a remarkably silent fight, lacking any of the war whoops and yells with which it had begun. They all seemed to be scrambling around and puffing and blowing without saying anything very much.

But he heard himself say something then, or rather shout in wordless pain, as the boy who had sat on his legs grabbed hold of one of his feet and twisted it hard so that it really hurt. And then Pete was there, shoving aside one assailant and punching angrily at the other.

"Get up, Derry, quick!"

He wriggled up and out, but there was no getting

away because the two of them were at Pete now; so then in a moment the four bodies, Peter and he and the two White Road boys, with another hovering, were twisting and wrestling to and fro on the damp spring grass, and writhing away from the hawthorn branches that reached out to scratch at their skin.

And so it might perhaps have gone on indefinitely, in a long, endless grubby confusion, if one or two or all of them had not glanced up out of their wrestling and seen Tom.

Derek only knew that somehow they all fell away from one another as if there had been a signal, and lay there panting and looking across at the wide clear patch of grass beside the thicket. He saw Geoff propped up on his elbows watching, too, and David Wiggs raising his head where he lay beside him, and two other White Road boys standing close by, loose-armed and still. And over in the open space, Tommy Hicks was standing facing Johnny Wiggs, the two of them alone.

They were both slightly crouched, with arms crooked and ready, like wrestlers waiting to spring. They were both disheveled and panting and spattered with clay, and there was no knowing whether all this came from the general rough and tumble or whether they had already been fighting there alone, the two of them. But that wasn't it, Derek thought, watching them. This was something about to happen. This was the bomb about to go off. His shoulders twitched in a sudden involuntary shiver, and he felt a prickling in his neck. But he could not keep his eyes off the wire-taut figures of the two big boys. None of them could. Wherever they stood or sat or lay, they were paralyzed into an audience, frozen in expectation and a kind of fear.

And then the bomb did go off. Johnny Wiggs lunged sideways at Tom and brought his back fist swinging forward, and Tom dodged so that the fist hit his arm, and dived with the same arm stretched out and pulled Johnny Wiggs off balance and down to the ground, where they rolled over and over in a horrible, furious confusion of flailing arms and kicking legs. Then somehow they were up again, weaving silently about in the same ominous pause as before. And then the heads came down and the arms swung, and Derek winced as he heard a muffled thump from Johnny Wiggs's fist connecting with part of Tom, and he ducked his head and shook it and felt sick. The fight went on, and they sat mesmerized, and as it went on, it grew worse and more bitter and malevolent, and Derek knew that each of the watching boys, both friend and enemy, felt as he did himself: caught up in a great unmanageable fear at the sight and sound of a fighting that was not like their own kind of fighting at all, but something much older and bigger and with emotions behind it of a kind they did not know. These two big boys were engaged in something that made him suddenly feel very small. He could hardly bear to look at their faces, each now and then visible for a flaring second out of the whirl of angry limbs or the wary, watchful circling that punctuated the scuffling bursts. The look on these faces was not a look he had ever seen on the face of any boy he had ever fought. He had glimpsed, often enough, plain anger and the vengeful concentration of wanting to hurt, but he had never seen this. This was

something different. Tom Hicks and Johnny Wiggs these two still were, but their faces had changed utterly; they were twisted up in some vast adult emotion as if they were fighting some fight that was not about themselves only, but about far bigger things. There was the sneer of real hatred on their faces. He had never seen hating before. He remembered Pete saying that the two had often fought, but even so, this looked like more than a kind of climax to years of enmity; almost as if the whole world had suddenly divided into two and

the two halves were here flinging themselves one against the other.

They were both big boys, and neither was showing any sign of tiring. The fight seemed to go on and on, the punching and the wrestling and the rolling over and around, and the boys watching began gradually to murmur like trees in the wind. Gazing, obsessed with the need for one or the other to win, they began to stir uneasily as their own champion was rocked by a blow, or to murmur in support if he landed a punch or twisted the other boy out of range; and listening, Derek found these sounds even nastier than the silence had been, and the more so because he knew he was making them himself.

It was Johnny Wiggs who brought the end of it, and he did it by breaking the silence: the silence that had seemed magical, a spell cast in such a way that so long as no sound was made, except a gasp or a wordless grunt, the fight would go on and on without end. Johnny Wiggs had begun to look as though he were winning; in their last long scuffle he had managed to hold Tom pinned down helplessly long enough to thump at him viciously several times and to send the breath gasping out of him and begin a trickle of blood from his nose. But at the last moment Tom had curved his back and given a great jerk, and tumbled Johnny Wiggs sideways into a particularly thorny bramble clump; and then they were apart again and stumbling, panting, to their feet.

They stood a yard or two apart, glaring, ready; but Tom was clearly winded by the last scuffle and swaying where he stood. Johnny Wiggs clenched his fists and bobbed lightly on the balls of his feet and laughed jeeringly at Tom with the confidence of the one who was about to win.

"Hey, sailor boy," he said softly. "Running out of steam, sailor boy? You're not much good, are you, sailor boy, not without your sailor suit? Need a nice uniform like Daddy's to prove what a brave boy you are."

In the group watching, David Wiggs laughed loudly, and his cronies sniggered; Derek felt his cheeks grow suddenly hot and saw Pete jump angrily to his feet. But before either of them moved, Tom moved, did more than move. He leaped at Johnny Wiggs with his mouth clenched tight and his eyes open very wide, and he seemed to shake him as a cat shakes a new-caught mouse before he hit him, once, very hard and very fast. Nobody saw the fist move or even land, but they heard a horrible clicking sound as Johnny Wiggs's jaw rammed shut, and they saw Tom's arm drop down, and Johnny Wiggs stagger for a moment and suddenly fall down in a heap on the ground.

Tom stood where he was, looking down, breathing heavily, and his face relaxed and smoothed itself out so that for the first time since the fight had begun, he looked like himself again. The boys from the White Road were murmuring like bees around Johnny Wiggs's prostrate form. Peter and Derek and Geoffrey hovered, fascinated and a little scared, behind them, and after a moment Tom shook his head as if to dislodge something from the top of it and came and stood over the group and pulled two of the boys aside. But at the same moment Johnny Wiggs groaned and put out an arm and pushed at the ground and sat up, rubbing his chin.

Perhaps if the two boys had spoken, or even looked at one another, it would have broken the spell. Perhaps it would have taken away the huge and awful strangeness of the mood that still hung over them all: the sense of something unfamiliar and frightening and impossible to understand. Perhaps. But before Johnny Wiggs could even raise his head and look up at Tom, before anyone could do anything, the silence and the sunshine and the whole spring day fell to bits, and out of nowhere into the sky there rose the thin climbing, growing wail of the siren that meant an air raid. Up in its wailing curve of distorted music it went, gathering strength as the note went higher, until it was shrieking its loudest along the waving line, *whooo—ooo—whoooo—ooo,* up, down, up, down, filling the sky, filling the ears, filling the whole world. And as Derek listened to it and flinched beneath it, he was afraid, and he knew he had never been afraid in this way in his life before.

He looked at the others, all the others who had been under the spell of the fighting, too, and he saw the same fear on every face.

He looked up at Tom, and Tom was looking at all three of them.

"Go home," Tom said. "Go on, it's a raid; you'll have to. Over the gate at the top of Everett. Go on now, run."

Everyone was scattering. Johnny Wiggs was up on his feet, shaking his head and rubbing the back of his neck, and with the White Road boys clustering around him, he began to move past the thicket toward the back of his house. Tom turned toward his own fence.

"He was smashing," Derek said softly, even through the alarm buzzing in his head.

"Mmm," Geoffrey said, and he meant it, but the noise of the siren was dissolving him. "Come on."

Peter stood still and called, "Tom!"

Tom glanced back over his shoulder.

"You won," Peter said.

Tom grinned at them and flapped both hands to wave them home. They turned to the gate of the field, and they found themselves face to face with David Wiggs. None of them had noticed that he was still standing there.

Nobody said anything. For a moment they stared. Then David Wiggs puckered his weaselly face and spat, viciously, at Peter's feet. And then he ran.

There was no time to do anything, and perhaps nothing to do even if there had been time. The siren was still pouring out its warning, and they felt urgently that they had to be away and at home before its last dying wail began the long prelude to the danger of the raid. Derek felt it now as he had never felt it before. "Come on," he said, and ran.

Over the gate that ended Everett Avenue, and its one strand of barbed wire that was really no hindrance after all; past Tom's house; down the road. Derek veered away from them to his own gate as the siren's note began dangerously to wail its way down.

"See you tomorrow!"

Geoff ran without seeming to hear, but Peter grinned over his shoulder and waved. "I'll call for you, Derry—be seeing you!"

But they did not see one another again that day. The first raid was not a long one and never came close; Derek and Hugh heard only very distant gunfire and did not even go down into the shelter, though Mrs. Brand kept them close to her and ready to run if there should be need. The all clear sounded after about an hour. Derek spent the rest of the day indoors, since his mother was still edgy, and played with Hugh. He was so shaken by the fight, and the strange feeling it had brought, that he was glad of the quiet house and the chance to build his small brother castles and towers of wooden bricks. It was a comfort, a proof that whatever might be prowling outside, his own world and the people closest within it were still secure.

He was in bed and asleep when the night raid came. He had not heard the siren, and he never knew how long the raid had been going on before he woke. There were so many thumps and bumps in the night outside that it might have been in progress for hours. He had been dreaming about the fight: an unpleasant, distorted dream in which Tom was fighting not the elder Wiggs but his brother David. Derek was watching with Peter, and suddenly the fight took a horrible mad turn, and the two who were fighting stopped punching one another and turned and came across to where Peter and Derek were sitting, and Tom looked down at them with that frightening face full of hate and said, "It's your turn now," and David Wiggs laughed, and then suddenly changed from laughing to the same hating face and spat on the ground at Peter's feet as he had during the real day. And Derek was swamped by an awful fear. It engulfed him as if he had jumped into a bottomless lake, and nothing else existed except the feeling of being horribly afraid.

And it was out of that fear that he woke into the noisy night, blinking in relief at the reality that was, in spite of the noise, so much better than the dream. But something of the fear stayed with him, whether from the dream or the day before, and he listened uneasily to his parents talking in low, concerned voices beside the door of the room.

"It's getting much closer," John Brand said. "I really think we should take them down to the shelter, Mary."

"Couldn't we try the cupboard under the stairs?" His mother sounded unhappy. "They say it's the safest place in a house. They'd be almost as safe there. It's such a cold night, and Hugh's cough—"

"I want you to be safe, too," his father said gently. Out of one half-open eye Derek saw him put his arm around Mrs. Brand's shoulders and give her a hug. "Come on now, wrap him in plenty of blankets. The Thermos is in the kitchen all ready. I'll get Derry up." Then he was bending over Derek and slipping an arm beneath his head. "Come on, old chap, wake up. We're going down in the shelter for a bit."

Struggling into sweater and shoes and dressing gown, Derek felt empty and sick with fear of the night and the noises it was making. He was still woozy with sleep, but the fear was there, very strong and unfamiliar, and he did not know how to handle it. As they went quickly out into the darkness, he held tightly to his mother's hand and looked up and saw the white crisscrossing arms of the searchlights sweeping the black sky, and small and far off the bursting stars of shells, and below and behind it all the red glow in the eastern sky, as if he were seeing them all for the first time.

In the small dank, earth-smelling box of the shelter, it was better at first, because they were all close together. Even though the noise outside grew steadily worse, Derek lay curled and relaxed and almost fell asleep. But at the pit of his stomach the fear still crawled. And all at once it jabbed him viciously as the roar of a diving plane shrieked out of the dull background of rumbling and thumps, and while it still filled his head, there were two great crashes somewhere close. He felt his bunk quiver, and he jerked upright and hit his head on the roof. He had a glimpse of his father's face, strained and intent.

Then the third explosion came, and it was as if the world had blown up. The noise poured through his head so that it sang in his ears even after he knew that it had stopped. He ducked automatically and stayed crouched with his head on his knees. He had never heard anything so shatteringly loud. His bunk and the whole shelter shuddered and shook, and outside in the night there was a sequence of other smaller, closer noises, noises of breaking and clattering and something that sounded like tiles falling from their own roof.

The shelter gave a second tremor much fainter than the first, and then the worst close noise was gone, and there was only the rumbling again and the sound of the guns, and Derek raised his head fearfully and stared at his mother and father in the dim light of the jumping candle flame. His mother reached up and took hold of his arm and held it tightly. "All right, love. All right." Blanket-bundled in her arms, Hugh whimpered, and she bent her head to murmur to him.

John Brand moved to the candle and pinched out its flame between his finger and thumb, then warily pulled the blackout curtain and the wooden cover over the shelter entrance a little way aside. Derek peered out at what little of the gap he could see, and gasped. The night was not dark now. It was a dusky red, and its light was strangely flickering.

His father turned back. He rattled a box of matches and gave it to Mrs. Brand, still holding the entrance open with one hand.

"Down the road," he said. "Looks like a direct hit. I shall have to go and help, love."

"Oh, John—" Mrs. Brand said, and her voice was shallow and quavering as Derek had never heard it before.

"Look," John Brand said, "it must have been the one plane. Off course from the factories, like last time. There's nothing else coming down. Not now."

"You don't know," she said.

"It might have been us," he said. "Thank God it wasn't. They need help. I'll be back as soon as I can." He kissed her quickly. "Stay down until the all clear goes." He pressed Derek's knee hard. "Look after them, Derry," he said.

"Be careful," Mrs. Brand said softly.

He went out, and Derek heard the rattle of the

wooden cover going back into place, and his father was gone.

His mother laid Hugh gently on the bunk, checked the blackout, and lit the candle again.

Derek said suddenly, his voice coming out high and hoarse, "Dad isn't going to get shot, is he, Mum?"

"Of course not, love," she said, and reached up and

hugged him. "He'll be very careful. But one of the houses down the road was hit by that last bomb. Daddy could see the fire. So everyone has to go and get the people out of the house before they get hurt."

The guns were still thumping, but the rumble of planes had died away. Derek looked at the candle flame, sending up its quivering black line of smoke, and lay back on his bunk. "Peter's dad will be helping, too," he said. "And Geoff's. They live closer to that end than we do. I expect Pete's dad was the first there. Whose house do you think it was, Mum? Old Mr. Graham at the end of the road?"

"I don't know, love," she said. "But I hope no one was hurt. Now you try to get some rest until the all clear goes. Hughie's asleep; we don't want to wake him up."

Derek thought: "The guns are still making as much noise as our talking is." But all the same he knew what his mother meant. People's voices were not usual, but small Hugh was used to the talking of the guns. They were a normal background to his sleep, every night.

His father had not come home when the all clear sounded. The sky was beginning to lighten with the dawn, and somewhere a single bird had begun to chirrup. Derek helped his mother back into the house with Hugh; then drank some cocoa with her in the kitchen, feeling strange and adult and unreal. Flames were still flickering down the road, and it did look as though they were coming from the Grahams' house. Old Mr. Graham was the sort of man to whom one always said good morning politely; he was thin and white-haired, but very upright, with a neat waxed moustache. He lived three doors away from the Hutchinses, and he had a plump and smiling wife whom they seldom saw. Derek wondered what they would do without their house. He thought: "Pete must have a good view."

Then he went dutifully to bed, leaving Mrs. Brand waiting in the kitchen, and his determination to stay awake dissolved as soon as he lay down and pulled up the bedclothes and felt his mother slip into the room and tuck him in. He fell asleep, and this time did not dream.

9

Wednesday

They told him in the morning, almost as soon as he woke up. The curtains were open, and around the sides of the guardian wardrobes the sun was slanting bright into the room. He sat up and looked across and saw a star-shaped cluster of cracks in the side window that had not been there the night before.

His mother and father came into the room, and his mother sat down beside him and took his hand, and John Brand stood awkwardly at the end of the bed and looked at them; and Derek looked at them both in astonishment and alarm and knew that something was very wrong.

"Darling," his mother said. "There is some very bad news. You must be a brave boy." Her hand clenched hard around his. "Derry darling, the house that was hit last night was Peter's house. Peter and his mother and his father and Miss MacDonald were all killed instantly by the bomb."

Derek sat very still. The rail at the end of his bed

was golden-brown where the sunlight was touching it.

"They didn't feel any pain," his mother said. "It was all over in a moment, and they couldn't even have known what was happening. The bomb fell right on top of the house."

Derek said, "Oh no." He wanted very much to say something else, anything else, but there was nothing else in his head to say. He thought of Pete coming up the road after breakfast to call for him, and found himself listening desperately for the knock on the door.

Mrs. Brand said gently, "Derry darling, it's very, very sad when people are taken away. It makes us very miserable, those of us who are still here. But Peter and Mr. and Mrs. Hutchins wouldn't like that, they wouldn't be happy if they knew we were very upset. So we have to try to be brave and think of them as we knew them. That's the way they would want it. Peter was such a sunny, happy boy." Her voice shook, and she stopped.

Hugh was standing up in his cot. "Oh no," he said. "Oh no, Mummy, oh no." He looked across the room happily for the laughter that he still occasionally got when he successfully copied something somebody else had said.

Derek said, "They slept in the Morrison shelter. They sleep there every night, Pete says; they even take their cat in. I saw it. It's under the table; it looks like a camp."

His father said, "It was a direct hit, you see. A Morrison can survive pretty well anything except a direct hit."

"Was Pete's cat killed, too?" Derek said.

He was not paying much attention to what he was saying. The misery and fright were growing inside him like a great swelling balloon. Yesterday the world had begun going badly wrong, but it was to have been better again when today came; the bits of nightmare could have been forgotten. But instead today had brought a change that would need more than forgetting. His world had stopped, and the world he would live in from now on would be a different world. The old one with Pete in it would never come back again.

Hugh banged the side of his cot and said again happily, "Oh no."

The day seemed to Derek to have no connection with reality. It was like a day in a dream from which they would surely, sometime soon, wake up. His father left the house soon after breakfast and was gone for the whole morning. A fire engine on its way home came up the road to turn around, and then went back again. There had been ambulances during the night, too, Mrs. Brand said. The houses on either side of the Hutchinses' had been badly damaged by the same bomb and people hurt and taken to hospital, but they would be all right in the end. She said nothing else about the bomb, and indeed she and Derek said very little else at all, but only stayed close together, playing with small, uncomprehending Hugh.

John Brand came home at midday looking dusty and sad. He picked Derek up and held him very tightly for a moment, and then he put him down and went into the kitchen. With half his mind listening and the other half attending to Hugh's prattling, Derek heard him say, "Well, it's all over. Nothing more to be done. Just one shaky wall left that they'll have to do something about pretty soon. It was very—complete. None of them could have known a thing." Then there was the hiss of a faucet being turned on, and no more words to be heard.

"None of them could have known a thing," Derek said to himself, and tried to realize that he was talking about Pete, and could not. He felt tight all over, as if his skin had suddenly become too small, and he kept catching himself wondering when Pete would come knocking at the door so that they could go up to the back field and start repairing the camp.

After their meal, when Hugh had gone protesting into the bedroom for his afternoon nap, Derek stood looking out of the front window, at the holly tree in which he and Peter had found the robin's nest the year before and deliberately failed to tell Geoff for fear he might take the eggs.

"Hey, Derry," his father said. "The sun's shining. Come into the garden and show me how well you're going to bowl this season."

"Daddy," Derek said. "Can I go and look at Pete's house?"

There was a silence behind him, and he turned from the window and saw them both looking at him, his father in the armchair by the fire and his mother standing by the door she had just come through, with the tray and its two cups of tea and the cozy-wrapped teapot for the refills later.

His mother said gently, "You'll see it sooner or later when we go past, darling. Do you really think you want to go specially, quite so soon?"

"There's nothing to see, Derry," John Brand said. "The house just isn't there anymore."

"I know," Derek said. "I don't want to look, I mean

not like that. I just want to go." He looked for words, but did not even know what it was he was trying to say. "I just . . . thought . . . I ought to. I just wanted." He swallowed hard, and stopped.

His parents looked at one another as if they were talking, though they said nothing; and then his father said, "All right. Put on a thick jersey; it's cold out. And promise me you won't go close. Bombed houses are dangerous; there are parts that fall down later on."

Derek nodded. His mother crossed to the chairs with the cups of tea. She said, carefully expressionless, "Don't stay more than a little while, darling."

"No," Derek said.

Conscious of every movement he made, as if he were watching somebody else, he dragged a heavy sweater over his head and went out into the road. The sun still shone, in and out of the bustling clouds, but there was a chill wind, and the cold bit at his face and hands and knees. He set off down the road, with his hands in his pockets and his toes scuffing at the stones, and the calm grass-fringed houses on either side and the patchwork of puddles in the road looked so totally the same as they had always looked that he did not believe that he would not arrive at Peter's front gate, and press the latch that was different from their own, and go past the hawthorn tree to the back door, and ring the bell and say to Mrs. Hutchins, as she looked with her unlaughing blue eyes, which might have been just shy, around the door, "Hallo, Mrs. Hutchins. Can Pete come out, please?"

But he was within sight of it now. The world was not normal after all.

The houses on either side, the Chants' and the Evanses', looked as though they had been hit by a gigantic fist; the Chants' house was only half standing, with its side broken away and the upper floor sticking out like a shelf, and a torn carpet hanging over the edge with a wardrobe standing on it almost ready to tumble off, both of them making the house look utterly naked, as if the life inside it had suddenly been brought defenseless into the open like an anthill cut open by a spade. The Evanses' house was not actually blown in half, but had all its windows broken and half the roof ripped away, so that only skeletal wooden beams remained. And the near wall was blackened by fire.

Peter's house, as John Brand had said, was not there.

Derek stood quite still, and stared. There was not even the ghost of a house, nothing that could be recognized: only a great pile of rubble, with a small triangular piece of brick wall standing up at the back of it; and upturned earth that looked for all the world like their pile of clay in the field, and the blackened groping roots of a tree, and scattered chunks of paving lying in a lot of water, as if the whole jumbled mass had been dropped into a pond. In spite of the water there was a strange, strong smell of dust. Bricks and broken beams were sticking out of the hole that had been the front garden, and the cherry tree that grew in the road outside the house was leaning out half uprooted with shattered bricks all around it. And Derek saw, then, one thing that he recognized and that told him this unimaginable chaotic ruin had indeed once been the

Hutchins house. He saw that the front gate was still there.

Though the low brick wall that had edged the garden had been blown out into a broken ridge of brick, the gateposts had held; they still stood there, leaning at strange angles away from one another, and from one post the gate hung half open: an entrance to nowhere. He stood there in the road looking at it, wide-eyed, appalled by the gate without knowing why. It was all wrong that it should be there; all wrong to be able to see it, or even open it, and not to be able to go through to everything that had always been there on the other side.

It was some time before he realized that there were other people in the road besides himself. Without properly looking, he glanced across at the other side. Two or three women were standing there talking, and a group of children. Then beyond them another figure came out of a gate farther up the road and ran down toward him. It was Geoff.

He slowed abruptly as he came close, and hesitated, and then came to stand at Derek's side.

"Hallo, Derry."

"Hallo."

They stood there in silence, looking at the rubble.

"My dad," Geoffrey said at last, and stopped and cleared his throat. "My dad said it must have happened awfully quick. Without them knowing."

Derek said, "So did mine."

He felt dull and stupid. There was nothing they could say to one another yet. They would have to learn to be friends in a new way, without Peter there as well. He said at last, "Were you all right?"

Geoffrey nodded. "Our front windows were all blown in," he said. "But we were down in the shelter next door."

Derek looked for the first time at the houses on the opposite side of the road, and saw that several of them were blind-eyed, with jagged-edged gaps where most of their windows had been. Slowly he realized that it must have been done by the blast from the bomb. He knew about blast: that was one of the reasons why you were supposed to get down on the ground if you were caught outdoors in a raid, because even if a bomb fell some way away from you, it could knock you down just the same. The houses near their school had lost their windows the same way. It had not occurred to him to consider any of the secondary effects of the bomb that had hit the Hutchins house.

He heard footsteps on the loose stones of the road and turned back again, seeing Geoff suddenly grim-faced and stiff. Another boy had come up to them and was standing there with one hand held oddly behind his back; standing nervous and irresolute, as if ready to turn back and run. It was David Wiggs, alone, with none of the White Road boys.

Derek looked at him in dull surprise. He was a long way from his own territory. Did he want to talk about fighting again? *Didn't he know?*

David Wiggs said, rubbing his nose nervously on his sleeve, "I been watching for you. I got something to give you." He brought his other hand slowly out from behind his back and held it out. "Here."

It was Peter's gun. The long dull-shining barrel, the revolving chamber, the carved black handle; Derek had not seen them since Peter had good-naturedly tucked the gun away with his darts and Geoff's birds' eggs in the secret cupboard of their camp. And then the next day the camp had been smashed into nothing, as Pete's house was now nothing, and the gun had been taken away.

He reached out and took it and held it in both hands, running one finger up and down the barrel. It was Pete's gun. Pete was really proud of his gun. He would have to make sure he gave it to Pete. He stared down at it, unable to look up, unable to say a word, and he heard David Wiggs shift from one foot to the other and kick unhappily at the ground. And suddenly the hard lump of misery that had been lying immovable inside Derek, and stopping him from thinking about tomorrow and the other tomorrows, seemed to explode up into his throat and fill his whole head and mind; and he gave a great sob. He tried to stop it coming again, ducking his head and holding the gun so hard that the metal bit into his fingers; but a second time the ugly, ripping sound jerked out of him. And he spun around and flung one arm toward David Wiggs in something that was half a blow and half a push, so that the boy staggered backward and almost fell on the stones; and then Derek was running, blindly, fast, stumbling to escape, not from the boy from the White Road but from the house, the house that was no longer there.

He ran up the road, through the stones and through the puddles, clutching Peter's gun, with the huge ugly sobs of his misery tearing themselves up from his chest. He ran in through the gate of his own house, through without pausing into the back garden; he scrambled through the loose planks in the back fence and lurched across the back field and the stile to the allotment land. Climbing the last fence before the Ditch with no one else to hold down the barbed wire, he slipped and gashed his leg, but it did not hurt.

Then he was down in the ruins of their shattered camp, where the splintered wooden boxes and fragments of eggshell still lay among the trampled mounds of clay. He looked wildly around him, still jerking with the strange deep noises over which he had no control; and he put down the gun, and snatched up one of the broken pieces of wood, and began furiously scraping out a shallow hole in the side of the Ditch below the place where Peter and he had buried the small dead cat. When the hole was big enough, he picked up Pete's gun and put it inside and pushed back the damp orange-brown clay to cover it, and then stamped it all down until no one could see where the hole had been.

And the sobs that were tearing him in half eased down, so that he could breathe without gasping, and under the cold sunshine of the April day he sat down in the ruin of the camp, and put his head on his knees, and cried.